MW01136364

Light of Devotion

~Men of the Heart: Book Four~

Steve C. Roberts

Men of the Heart - Book Four

Light of Devotion

Steve C. Roberts

Also By Steve C. Roberts

Non-fiction

Mighty Men: Lessons for the Christian Soldier

One Minute Thoughts: A Daily Devotional

Seven Steps to a Successful Christian Life
Lessons in Faith

Like a Tree Planted

Fiction

~Men of the Heart Series~

Kindled Love – Book 1

Sparks of Affection – Book 2

Flames of Endearment – Book 3

Light of Devotion – Book 4

~Other Fiction~

Flight Cancelled: A Christmas Romance

*Look for: A Walk in the Park: A Christmas
Romance (Spring 2020)*

Text Copyright © 2019 by Steve C. Roberts

Cover Design © 2019 by Elizabeth Roberts

Photographs from the Public Domain, Bureau of Land Management:

BLM Office: Wyoming

BLM Office: Oregon/Washington

All Rights Reserved. No part of this publication may be reproduced, stored in a retrieval system or transmitted in any form or by any means without the prior written permission of the publisher.

All Scripture Quotations are from the King James Version (1611)

Poetry Selections from:

The Giaour, A Fragment of a Turkish Tale—Lord Byron, 1813

Endymion—John Keats, 1818

This is a work of fiction. Names, Characters, Places and Incidents either are the product of the authors imagination or are used fictitiously, and any resemblance to actual persons, living or dead, business establishments, events or locales is entirely coincidental.

Special thanks to my amazing wife, and daughters—who have earned the dubious honor of being the first readers.

Thanks also to all of my dedicated readers who have been waiting patiently for this to finish.

PART I

PROLOGUE

Philadelphia, PA—1871

"Stupid wench!" Horace yelled loudly as he picked up the settee. "You don't talk to me like that!" He flung it hard, and Rosemary barely ducked in time; the settee missed her and smashed into the wall.

Rosemary glanced over to where Sarah stood cowering in the corner. She could see the trail of tears streaking down her face—only five minutes ago they had been happily baking bread for dinner.

But then Horace had come home from the saloon.

Her eyes cut back over to Horace. He had paused after flinging the settee at her and was taking another long drink of his bottle. She wondered if he was done for the night. Sometimes he would...

He pulled the bottle away from his mouth, spilling liquor over the front of his shirt as he gestured with the bottle. "You ungrateful wretch. I don't know why I ever took you in!"

The words stung, but not as bad as the bottle did when it flew across the room and hit her in the face. She hadn't expected it and never had the chance to avoid it. A stinging blow and then she woke up on the floor. She hadn't even felt herself fall. Rosemary lifted her head slowly; Horace was still yelling, but now he had Sarah backed in the corner beating her with his belt—her cries mingled with the sound of blood rushing through her ears.

Rosemary looked back at the floor and her eyes focused on a small pool of blood where her head had been. She absently acknowledged it was hers and tried to sit up. She needed to help Sarah—she had to help Sarah—but the pain was making her slow...

She forced herself to her feet. Horace was yelling something about money as he continued to beat Sarah. She had to stop him. Finally making it to her feet, she lurched forward into Horace. "Leave her alone!" She grabbed him by his shoulder and tried to wrestle the belt from him, but he flung her back effortlessly.

He didn't usually go after Sarah—she was young still, only three and a half. He usually saved his violence for her and left Sarah out of it.

Horace hadn't always been violent. Before they were married—and even the first few days after—those days had been good. He'd first come around right after Ma and Pa died. A police officer had come by threatening to take Sarah to the orphanage. She had sat there and cried. Her closest neighbors had been out of town, she didn't know what to do, where to go, or who to turn to.

Then Horace had come to her, claiming to be a concerned neighbor. He had patted her shoulder and offered a proposal—marry him, and she'd be able to keep Sarah with her.

She hadn't been interested in marriage—after all, she was just seventeen—but Horace had sworn it was on paper only... just legal like, to keep the court from taking Sarah. He had seemed so nice and helpful, so as a last resort she had agreed.

And to be honest, it was nice at first. He was sweet and nice—until he was sure he had the house, and Pa's money.

Then, the drinking started. And that was when the beatings began.

The first time he'd hit her had been a surprise. Sarah had made a mess on the floor, and when Horace came in, he started yelling at her. When she had stepped forward to stop him from yelling at Sarah, he'd swung a backhanded blow that knocked her to the floor and told her to clean it up. She'd been so startled that she immediately cleaned up the mess and hid in her and Sarah's room the rest of the night. She couldn't believe he'd hit her. Even her Pa had never treated her like that.

The next morning Horace had apologized. He said he couldn't help it, but she'd made him do it by not keeping the house like she was supposed to. He said if she did what she was supposed to, it wouldn't happen again.

But then it not only happened again, it got worse. And now...

She shook off them memories as she struggled back to her feet, still dazed from the blow to her face. Sarah had stopped screaming and was just huddled in the corner, absorbing the blows as Horace continued beating her with the belt.

Rosemary knew she had to do something.

She staggered to the mantle. She had to stop Horace before he killed Sarah.

****** ******

Rosemary stood silently, staring at Horace's still form as a growing pool of red ran out from under his body. Sarah was standing now, staring at her dully. Her mouth was moving, but all Rosemary could hear was a loud ringing in her ears. Her arms felt like lead weights and she looked down, confused, realizing with shock that she was holding her Pa's shotgun in her hands. She dropped it like it was red hot and stared down at it for several seconds as understanding dawned on her.

She'd shot Horace. Now she was going to hang.

She made up her mind in a brief second. She ran and picked up Sarah, clutching her close to her chest as she ran for the bedroom. She had been thinking about leaving for weeks, since the beatings had become unbearable. She'd already had a plan, and even had a small bag and some money hidden so she could go. She'd just never been brave enough.

Now courage was immaterial. She had to run for her life.

With Sarah still clutched in her arms, she bent down and rummaged under the bed for the bag. She gritted her teeth as her head swam and little lights burst in her vision, but she needed the bag. She had an extra dress for herself and one for Sarah, as well as some other odds and ends.

As soon as she pulled it out, she ran for the back door, pausing only to grab Sarah's coat. Her hearing was starting to return, and she could hear Sarah's sobs. She knew it wouldn't be long before the neighbors showed up, or worse yet, the police... she had to get out fast.

Her first thought was of the railroad. She could get on a train like those hobos did. She could get on and get away... far away.

She opened the door and peeked out. The backyard was empty as far as she could see, but she could hear *a faint banging on the front door. She knew she didn't have long.*

With a final parting glance at Horace's still body, she slipped out into the night.

****** ******

Rosemary staggered down to the train tracks clutching Sarah and the small bag. She didn't know how quickly the police would start chasing her, but she knew she needed to get as far away as she could.

She reached the tracks and started following them out of town. There were trains that passed through town in the night, and she hoped to catch one of them—she just couldn't sit around at the depot waiting. That would be the easiest way to get caught.

By the time the town lights faded behind her, Sarah had fallen into a fitful sleep... Rosemary shifted her and continued walking. She needed to stop and rest but wanted to be far away before that happened. A partial moon was out, and it was bright enough for her to see where she was going. She walked another half-hour—she was guessing she was two or three miles from town when she finally stopped to rest and listen for pursuit.

She strained to listen, but all she could hear was that incessant ringing in her ears.

It was then that the full import of what she had done hit her. She'd killed a man.

Rosemary felt herself start to shake and sat down heavily on the side of the tracks, still clutching Sarah tightly in her arms. It wasn't just about hanging. It was the idea that she had killed someone.

Every Preacher she'd ever heard said that killing someone would send you straight to hell... but she'd had to stop Horace. He might have killed Sarah if she hadn't...

No. She tightened her jaw, wincing slightly at the pain that shot through the side of her face. Preacher had to be wrong. God wouldn't be mad at her for saving Sarah.

She nodded curtly to herself and forced herself to her feet. No, she was sure she was fine with God... It was the police she had to worry about now, and she needed to get as far away from them as she could. Grimacing through the pain, she staggered down the tracks, heading further away from town. When she had walked another half-hour, her arms felt like they were ready to fall off her body, and her legs were about to collapse.

She pushed through the brush on the side of the tracks and laid Sarah down next to a big tree. She started to sit by her, but the ringing in her ears had settled down to where she could hear water bubbling over rocks somewhere nearby. She pushed deeper into the woods and found a small creek that was only a few dozen feet away from the tracks. She bet down and splashed some water on her face—the cold water stung her battered cheek—and then took a long drink before sitting back and staring at the water. The moon was shining in small streamers through the trees, glimmering off the surface of the water. It was so peaceful and calm here.

She wondered what time it was. She had her Pa's pocket-watch in her bag, but she had left that by Sarah—not that there was enough light to see it by right now anyway. She shook her head, it didn't matter. She was exhausted. She needed to sleep. The long walk carrying Sarah had taken everything out of her.

She stood stiffly and moved back to where she'd left Sarah. The little girl was curled up in a fetal ball, sleeping soundly. Rosemary sat heavily and curled up next to her sister. She would rest for a few minutes and then push on when she felt better.

****** ******

It was hours later when Rosemary woke up. She tried to open her eyes but could only manage to get the left one open. Her right eye was swollen shut, and tender to the touch.

She shifted slightly, not wanting to disturb Sarah. The little girl was snoring softly on the ground next to her. Rosemary carefully shifted and stretched her shoulder. She listened to her sister for a few moments but didn't dare disturb her; Rosemary knew the best thing for Sarah was to sleep.

As she lay there, she was surprised by the conflicting emotions she felt. There was a certain level of fear. Not simply fear of getting caught, but for what would happen to Sarah if they were caught. Other than that, she felt nothing... and somehow that was what bothered her the most—like there was a part of her that was missing.

There was a long whistle in the distance as a train passed through town.

She sat up slowly and looked around, wincing as pain shot through her head. Her entire body was stiff and sore; whether from the beating or the cool night air she didn't know, but it really didn't matter. She needed to move. She needed to get Sarah on that train.

She clambered slowly to her feet and nudged Sarah until she woke up. "Come on, Sarah, we need to get going."

The young girl stirred and sat up, obviously confused by the darkness. Rosemary found her hand in the dark and helped her to her feet. "We have to get back down to the train tracks."

They stumbled slowly through the darkness toward the train tracks, and Rosemary found herself wishing they hadn't gone as far into the woods to hide.

They reached the edge of the trees, and Rosemary peered out, scanning the area for movement. The partial moon was low on the horizon, casting an eerie glow on the empty tracks. She could hear the train engine now as it came up the hill out of town.

She felt a tugging at her coat and knelt down next to her sister. "Alright, Sarah, we're waiting here for a minute, and then we're going for a ride."

The train grew even closer, and she could see its bright lights as it chugged up the hill toward them. She pulled Sarah close and waited as the front of the train came closer. She could see men in the engine car and waited until it had passed before stepping out and moving toward it.

Luckily, it wasn't going very fast—barely faster than she could walk—so she moved to the side of the tracks, looking for some way onto the train. The cars that were going by were big boxes and there were some that had their doors slightly open. She chose one of those and waited for it to come abreast of where they stood, picking Sarah up as it approached. It was then that she noticed the train was starting to pick up speed.

Rosemary walked quickly to keep pace with the open door and pushed Sarah up into the slow-moving rail car. She didn't know how long they would be able to ride. She'd heard stories about conductors throwing hobos from fast-moving trains and had no interest in finding out if they were true. She simply hoped they could get as far away as possible before the police caught up with her.

She got Sarah inside, clambered in after, and then collapsed on the rough wood floor.

A sharp tug on her sleeve caught her attention, and she looked down in the dim light. Sarah was sitting next to her, her nose wrinkled as she pinched it with her finger and thumb.

Rosemary sniffed lightly before nodding to the small girl, "Yes, Sarah, I know it smells funny in here, but it's safe and that's what matters." She was pretty certain they had used these cars to haul cattle before, but it was better than the alternative.

She stood and worked the door shut. She didn't want enough light for Sarah see her face at the moment. She could tell that it was swollen, and she was worried that after everything that happened with Horace, seeing her would make Sarah relive the horror of...

Well, that.

She pulled Sarah close and they sat down against the wall of the train car. She listened closely to the clatter of the wheels over the spaces in the track as the train picked up speed. She smiled grimly, knowing that each clack symbolized a growing distance from danger. It wasn't long before she could hear Sarah's slow breathing that signaled she was asleep. It wasn't long before she felt herself drifting off to sleep.

****** ******

Rosemary woke suddenly to a sharp sound. She looked around the dimly lit car. Sunlight was filtering in through the cracks, so she knew she had been asleep for some time. After listening for several seconds, she realized the sound was the squealing of brakes as the train slowed.

She knew that, so far, she and Sarah had been lucky. She just hoped their luck continued. As she stared at the wall, she made a decision. She wasn't going to stop. She would take Sarah all the way west... to California. No one would ever find them there. They could start a new life with new names...

She had plenty of money—almost a hundred and fifty-dollars. She grinned lopsidedly; Horace would have beside himself if he'd known how much money she'd hid from him. With that much, she could go almost anywhere and do almost anything.

So, as the train slowed, she stood with a new level of determination driving her. Everything was going to be alright.

****** ******

ONE

Japheth Nathaniel Taylor stared stupidly at the hat he had clutched in his right hand. It was Jed's hat, and he had no idea why he had picked it up. He shook his head to clear it. His ears were ringing loudly, and there was a droning noise in the background—like someone yelling across the room—but the ringing was so loud he couldn't figure out what they were saying.

He cut his eyes over to Jed, who was lying sprawled out with his legs folded at a weird angle. That was how he'd landed after the bank teller let him have both barrels of his scattergun.

Shaking his head once more, he looked up, meeting the eyes of the elderly woman with the small silver derringer. She had cut Simmons down at close range—Simmons, who had boasted about being the fastest gun in the west—he surely hadn't drawn faster than that schoolmarm. Now he was lying dead against the wall only a few feet away, and his pistol hadn't even cleared leather.

He drug his eyes over to the Sheriff, who was standing across the room calmly thumbing shells into his pistol. He'd emptied it when he'd shot Hank to doll rags.

Japheth looked back down at the hat in his right hand. He'd dropped his own pistol when the scattergun had blown Jed across the room, and when he'd reached down to pick it up, he'd came up with the hat instead.

Which had likely saved his life. If he would've come up holding that pistol, they would've probably dropped him as well.

But they'd hesitated when he stood up unarmed, and that was all the room he'd needed. He snapped into action and ran out of the bank as fast as his legs could carry him.

As he ran for his horse, the thought raging through his mind was why. Not why he was running for his life—the bullets flying toward him answered that question—but the more important why. Why had he been riding with those fools to begin with? At this point he couldn't have supplied anyone with a good reason.

It wasn't about drinking and carousing around, because the only time he'd ever had liquor was when he and little Jonny Tulle had snuck out back of the woodshed with his grandma's Rheumatiz' medicine.

He'd taken one sip, broke out in hives, and collapsed to the ground. His Pa had run for the town Doctor who said he had 'bout died 'cause he was allergic to the liquor. Of course, his Pa tried to make it twice in a row, 'cause when he'd healed up, his Pa took him out back of that same woodshed once more... that time with a switch.

Point of fact; that was the one and only time he'd ever had liquor.

As far as the carousing around, he'd promised his Ma on her deathbed that he wouldn't even hold a girl's hand 'til they were married, and he was fairly certain that his Ma would come back from the grave to skin him alive if he didn't keep that one.

He supposed that the only reason he was with them was because they were young and full of spirit. When he'd come west there were young men and old men— the old men talked about the past, and the young men talked about themselves—he guessed it was more exciting to talk about himself with the rest of them.

Either way, it looked like he'd ended up with the wrong fools and was about to pay for it with his life.

He reached his horse and jumped on, suddenly realizing that he had that bag of gold still clenched in his left hand. He'd dropped the hat at some point but had kept ahold of the bag—and he didn't see any sense in letting loose of it after all of that trouble, so he gripped the reins with his right hand and let out a loud *WHOOP*, and his appaloosa took off like a shot.

By the time his horse hit the town limits, people were pouring out of the bank. More importantly, they were shooting rapidly in his direction. He could almost feel the bullets whizz by him, but he didn't slow down.

He rode hard without looking behind him for several miles before slowing his horse to a quick trot. Looking back, he couldn't see any sign of pursuit, but that didn't mean it wasn't there. He figured he just had a little lead on them and needed to keep his horse as fresh as possible.

He kept the horse at a quick trot for a while, looking back every time he topped out on a hill to see if the posse was coming.

The afternoon slowly passed as he rode, and the sun was heading down toward the horizon behind him when he spotted the dust cloud. He pulled his horse to a stop, stood up in the stirrups, and squinted into the distance. The posse was maybe five miles away and riding hard to catch him.

He yanked the reins and spurred his horse forward, putting him into a hard run for a good mile or so...

Right until he spotted the Ute war-party on the hill to his left. Clenching his jaw, he turned slightly south to avoid them, hoping their attention was focused somewhere else—like maybe that posse.

Hank had mentioned something about renegade Ute's in the area, but he hadn't paid much heed since the Indians were out here and he was in town and safe. No big deal.

Now it was a big deal.

He slowed to a trot to keep the dust down and rode for another mile before hooking back to the north. He figured if the Ute's gave chase, they might try to cut him off. By swinging 'round behind them, they would miss him. At least, that was his plan... but he'd only rode north for a few minutes before he saw smoke, and he knew after seeing that Ute war party, whatever the source of the smoke was, it wouldn't be good.

He found the source a few minutes later and pulled his horse to a stop at the top of a small rise looking down into a low valley.

Nine ravaged wagons were spread out below him in complete disarray. Several of them were burning, and the settler's belongings were strewn across the valley. It looked like the Ute's had hit the wagon train by surprise, which was puzzling, given that wagon trains usually had scouts out to check for danger.

He studied the scene closely; it looked like they had tried to make a stand. He could tell by their position that they had attempted to pull into a circle, but the spot they were caught in was in a small valley, and almost indefensible.

He reached down and touched the empty holster at his side, wishing once again that he had his pistol. He didn't even have a rifle, which left him completely defenseless. He didn't see any movement, but that didn't mean much. He knew the Ute's probably weren't done yet. They likely had scouts that had spotted the posse and would deal with them before coming back to finish looting the wagons.

He rode down the hill slowly toward the wagon train. If he were lucky, he might find a rifle or something that he could use and get away before the Ute's got back.

But as he reached the bottom of the hill, he almost turned his horse and went the other way. There were bodies laid out everywhere; both Ute and settlers. He'd seen a few dead bodies in his life, but nothing that prepared him for this.

Clenching his jaw to keep from vomiting, Japheth rode around the corner of a burned-out Conestoga, and that was when the firing started. The first round hit the pommel of his saddle, and he jerked back, shaking his feet loose of the stirrups as he kicked backwards off his horse. He hit the ground rolling as three more rounds punched into his horse, and it dropped screaming to the ground.

He crawled away from the Conestoga, stopping in the shadow of another wagon before coming to a low crouch... just as a Ute came out from behind the wagon.

Before he had time to react, the Ute leapt on top of him. They hit the ground rolling, and he elbowed the brave in the face and rolled to his feet as the Ute came up with a wicked looking knife in his hand.

Despite the situation, Japheth grinned because this was the kind of fight he liked.

His Pa had been a boxer and had taught him how to fight before he went off to the war. After his Pa left, there had been many times when Japheth needed to use his fists to keep himself out of trouble... Well, deeper trouble.

At this stage in is life, Japheth not only knew how to use his fists, but more importantly, he had plenty of strength behind them to make it all count.

So, when that Ute came at him with the knife, he faked a left and laid the brave out with a right to the jaw—and then remembered there was another one out there with a gun.

The second one tackled him from behind, slamming him into the side of the burning wagon. Heat seared at his face as he fought to get out of the fire. Japheth threw an elbow back hard and felt a sick crunch as it landed.

The figure went limp, and Japheth clambered quickly to his feet, shoving the body from him. Searing heat in his arm showed him that his shirt sleeve was on fire. He watched the Ute warily as he pounded the fire on his sleeve out. He could tell by the way the Ute stared up at the sky that the he wasn't moving ever again. He spat on the ground next to the lifeless Ute, suddenly annoyed. He'd just bought the shirt back in Klein before they robbed the bank. Now his arm hurt, and his shirt was ruined.

He looked back at the other Ute—the one he'd punched. He was unconscious, but his chest was moving, which told him the Indian was still alive. Japheth knew he should just kill him and be done with it but didn't have the stomach to kill an unconscious man, even if he had just murdered a bunch of settlers. Of course, he didn't want the Indian to sneak up on him either. He needed something to defend himself.

Japheth moved over to the closest body. It was a young man lying face up, his lifeless eyes staring at the sky. Japheth felt a shiver run through him—the man was about his age and wearing the same shirt as he was, red plaid.

It was a stark reminder of how close he had come to being laid out on a slab himself.

He shook off the thought and grabbed the pistol from the man's hand. He quickly checked the cylinder—all six rounds had been fired as the man tried to fight off the attack.

It took the same round as his pistol had, but he crouched down by the body and replaced the spent shells from the other man's belt. He didn't know how many rounds he would need before he got to safety. Once it was loaded, he stood and breathed a sigh of relief as he holstered the pistol. Now that he was armed, he felt safe... well, safer.

He looked over at the unconscious Ute. He needed to take care of him and get moving.

He grabbed the Ute's knife and walked back over to his fallen horse. His lips tight, he stared at the beast. He'd only had the horse for a few weeks but had really liked its spirit. Shaking his head sadly, he knelt and cut the reins from the bridle. As he stood, he noticed the spilled bag of gold on the ground next to the horse. He leaned over and picked up a piece, amazed that so many men had died for something so small and unprofound.

Shaking his head, Japheth stood, dropping the coin to the ground. He wanted no part of it. None of it.

Not anymore.

Moving quickly back to the unconscious Indian, he tied the Ute up, hoping the knots would hold the Indian long enough for him to get away.

Once he had the Indian secure, he started to move off, but a noise caught his attention and he stopped, listening intently, fairly certain that he wasn't alone.

Over the crackling of fire, he could hear soft sobs from somewhere nearby.

He drew his pistol and moved slowly toward one of the other wagons. He cocked the pistol and peered in, pausing when a voice spoke from the shadows.

"Are they gone?"

Japheth tensed and lifted the pistol before realizing it was a woman's voice. He peered deeper into the back of the wagon. The woman was pressed back against a large trunk.

More importantly, she was clutching a knife with both hands; holding it like a shield between them.

Lowering his pistol, he leaned in and whispered, "Are you alright?"

"Are they gone?" She asked again... the panic was unmistakable in her voice, and as he peered closer, he could see her eyes wide with terror.

"I just..." He paused, not really wanting to admit he'd just killed a man, even if it was an Indian that had just killed her friends. "Well, I took care of the last two that were here. The rest took off west toward a..." he trailed off again. How would he explain the posse out there? "Well, toward some other riders to the west."

"Will they be back?"

He blew out a breath, "Yes'm. I'm afraid they will." He cast a quick glance around. "It would probably be an idea to get moving." He held out his hand to help her out of the wagon.

She didn't move. "I have my daughter with me."

Snap. Japheth frowned and looked around, "Alright. We can get her out too." He looked back to the woman, "Do you have a gun?"

"No." Her voice shook with emotion, "I have a knife."

He nodded slowly, "Ok, wait here. I need to find us a horse."

He stepped back, mentally berating himself for checking the wagon. How was he going to get away with extra baggage?

He shook off the thought. He was probably the only chance that woman and her kid had of surviving, because if the Ute's came back, it was all over for them. He hurriedly circled the area, almost crying in relief when he spotted a small brown horse tied to the back of the far wagon. It was still saddled and had probably belonged one of the settlers from the wagon train. He supposed one of the two Ute's had kept it for himself—not that he was going to need it now—which is why it was still tied up. He moved closer, slowing as the horse nervously nickered. "Whoa, boy... settle down." He patted the horse's neck to calm it before grabbing the reins. Once the horse calmed, he quickly untied it and led it back to the wagon the woman was hiding in.

She hadn't moved from her spot in the wagon. He stood a few feet back and called softly, "Ma'am?"

She poked her head out from the wagon, "Yes?" Her voice was trembling with fear.

"I found one horse. It won't carry three people, but if you and your daughter can get up on it, I'll lead you out." He looked around, "I'm gonna check the rest of... well, through the other wagons and grab a few things while you get ready."

He moved quickly through the wagon train, checking the few wagons that weren't actively burning as he scanned the bodies for any signs of life as he gathered a few supplies and jammed them into a sack. The Ute's hadn't looted much yet—there were a few trunks that were opened, their contents spread out, but that was all—it looked like they had barely started before riding off toward the posse.

He grabbed a couple of blanket rolls off the top layer of a trunk and paused, considering the pile of clothing that lay underneath. Shrugging, he grabbed one of the shirts, a black one that looked about his size. He changed quickly, then with a second thought also grabbed a coat from the top of the trunk. He continued moving through the wagons, breathing a sigh of relief when he finally spotted a rifle on a fallen horse. He gladly took it, surprised that the Ute's hadn't grabbed it, as well as the saddlebags from the horse. He just hoped it had an extra box of shells for the rifle but didn't want to take time to look right then.

In the distance, he caught the rolling sound of gunfire. He stopped to listen for a few seconds as the shots echoed across the plains. It sounded like the posse had met up with the Ute's. He wondered who was going to come out on top.

Not that it really mattered. Either one would be a problem for him if they stuck around.

Japheth tightened his jaw and jogged back over to the wagon where the woman was. She had moved to the back, watching him closely as he untied the horse and held it by the reins. He looked around impatiently—they needed to get moving—then focused back on the woman, seeing her clearly for the first time. She looked young, maybe his age. "Are you ready to go, Ma'am?"

She nodded slowly, "I'm Mary, and this is my daughter." From behind the woman a small head peered out; a young girl, maybe three or four years old.

"I'm... uh..." He thought quickly, "Nathaniel... call me Nate." He wanted to slap himself for his stupidity. His middle name wasn't exactly the best cover out there, but it would have to do for now. He offered his hand, "But, we can talk later... we need to go." He gestured to the horse, "We've only got the one horse, so if you and your daughter can ride, I'll lead the horse out."

She took in a big breath and nodded as she climbed out of the wagon. The little girl clambered out after her mother and stood by her, waiting.

"Ma'am..." Nate offered his hand, but she ignored it and climbed up into the saddle, sitting awkwardly sideways with her dress. Once she was settled, he lifted the little girl up into her mother's arms. The child clutched her mother in a death grip that assured him that she wouldn't fall off.

The small horse had waited patiently throughout the mounting. In a way, he was glad it wasn't the appaloosa, which would have immediately started bucking at the unfamiliar riders.

Satisfied they were secure; Nate led the horse slowly through the wash and up the hill away from the burning wagons. The woman, Mary, had her daughter's face hidden as they moved through the wagons, trying to protect her from the scene of destruction and death.

But he was more concerned with how long it would be before either the posse or the Ute's arrived. He pulled the reins, wincing at the sharp pain that ran through his arm. The burn on his shoulder was still throbbing, and he was tired. He would rather have been riding the horse, but there was no room with both Mary and her daughter up there.

He sighed and cast a quick glance back. It looked like his company was going to be a much bigger problem than his shoulder. Here he was, not only on the run, but now he was going to have to play nursemaid to a woman and a kid as they passed through hostile Indian territory. He'd have to get them to the nearest town, other than Klein, and drop them off. To do that he would need to avoid hostile Indians, avoid a hostile posse, and with few supplies travel at least sixty or seventy miles.

He shook his head and continued walking.

***** ******

Mary's arms shook as she clutched Clara to her chest, swaying gently in the saddle as the man led the horse up the small hill. She wanted to comfort her sister but didn't trust her voice to speak after the horror of the past few hours. Everyone she'd been traveling with was dead, and they were at the mercy of a complete stranger.

Just when she'd thought they were home free.

She struggled for self-control as hot tears streamed down her face. Sarah... Mary shook her head, mentally reminding herself once again that her sister went by Clara now. Clara had sat in wide eyed terror throughout the attack. Mary had known her sister was terrified, even if she couldn't verbalize it.

Which she truly couldn't—Clara hadn't spoken a single word in six months... ever since Horace...

They had been traveling slowly westward toward California. The trip had taken longer and cost more than she'd initially thought it would. The money that they started with had, at first, seemed like a fortune, but just making it to St. Louis had taken most of it, and that was only a third of the journey. The rest of the trip would have taken more than they had left, and even if they had made it to California, would've left them with nothing.

They had stopped in Missouri for a while, and she worked in a laundry while helping a widow woman with sewing jobs. She had scrimped and saved for the last five months before finally taking this next step. She had been so excited when she'd met the Rothards, Hebert and Sally, who'd invited her to travel with them. It had seemed like the perfect setup; she would be a companion and help to Sally—who was due to have her baby very soon—and it would cost much less than traveling alone, leaving them plenty of money for the things they needed.

Plus, no one would think twice about her and Clara if they were with the Rothards.

She'd put almost all of her money into the trip... new clothes, new everything...

And now it was all in ashes. Everything but the small handbag she'd started her journey with.

She clutched Clara closer and wept bitterly, hoping the man wouldn't hear her.

***** ******

TWO

Near Medicine Bow, Wyoming

"How much further are we riding today?" Wilfred's whiny voice broke the easy silence the group had been riding in for the past few hours.

Tom Milburne sighed as he glanced back at the riders spread out behind him. "We'll pull up in a bit." He shook his head and focused back on the trail. It had been a long ride from Evanston, but they still had plenty of time to get to Wolcott.

He wasn't fond of the men he rode with, especially Wilfred, but that didn't really matter in their line of work—not that most people would really call it work, but that was alright.

He huffed out a quiet laugh. He really didn't trust any of them either, but he needed them to get this job done.

Well, technically the next two things done. He'd need their help to get Slade out, and he needed them and Slade to get that safe in Rawlings, which they had been heading for when Slade went and got caught in Evanston. Slade's brother had picked a fight over a card game, and it had went south quickly. Now Murphy was dead, and Slade arrested.

That had definitely disrupted their plans.

He'd been riding with Slade for almost three years. He liked Slade. Overall, he was usually levelheaded and made good decisions for the group. He just got caught in a bad place when his brother started trouble. Then when the Sheriff showed up with that wanted poster...Tom shook his head. It was lucky the lot of them hadn't got caught.

He noticed a small brook coming up ahead and angled to the side of the trail, guiding his horse down the small embankment before pulling up. He grimaced as he stepped from the saddle—it had been a long ride, and he was ready to relax for a while.

"Whadda ya think, Tom? You really wanna stop here?"

Tom looked up at Purvis, who was still perched on his horse eyeing him curiously. He nodded at the sun, still fairly high in the sky. "Plenty of time 'til sundown."

"You plannin' on camping out tonight?" Wilfred had drawn up at the top of the embankment and was looking around. "I'm hungry, and I'm tired of your cooking." Wilfred groused sullenly as he looked at the others. "I'm tired of being on the trail. I want to eat some real food, and sleep in a real bed."

Tom frowned and watched Wilfred closely. He was always making things difficult, mainly because he didn't like it when Tom was in charge, which was anytime Slade wasn't around. He shook his head, "We're still a ways off from Wolcott, but we don't want to ride in before Monday."

"Yeah." Jeffries interrupted, "We don't want to make Wolcott too early. People'd get suspicious to see all of us waiting around."

Tom nodded slowly, glad Jeffries had his back.

Miller spoke quietly from the back of the group, "There's a town a tad south of here. Probably a good hours ride anyway. Me and Purvis passed through it last year. It was pretty quiet..." He paused, then added, "...had good food too."

Tom lifted an eyebrow, "Law?"

Miller scrunched up his face, "Weren't none then, but that may have changed."

Tom sighed and nodded slowly. "Alright. We'll head there and rest before moving on."

***** ******

Cobbinsville, Wyoming

Parson William Stone took a slow sip of his coffee as he looked around the small restaurant. He'd had come into town early to run some errands and make a few visits but had finished earlier than expected. Now he was just wasting time until the stage came in.

He sat his cup down and glanced at the envelope that was sitting on the table. It was addressed to his wife's father, Tilman Boster. It had been several years since Anna had been in contact with her parents, and he'd finally convinced her to write them.

He smiled grimly. It had been an unspoken agreement between him and Anna for the past several months; he wouldn't bring up her relationship with her parents if she didn't bring up his relationship with his father—but now that his relationship with his father had been restored, he'd been pushing her to contact her family.

And after several weeks of pressure, he had finally succeeded.

He glanced down at the envelope once more as he took another sip of his coffee. The letter was brief and to the point. She'd given a brief explanation of what had happened over the past few years and encouraged them to write back. Short and to the point.

His mouth twitched in irritation, and he took another sip of coffee. Some people just confused him. Anna hadn't heard from them for almost ten years. They hadn't checked on her or even tried to contact her.

He hated to compare it to his own situation but always seemed to find himself unconsciously doing so. He had experienced a strained relationship with his father and had no interest in hearing from him. He had been on the move for years, but his father had still tried to find him, still tried to reach out...

Anna had been a widow for almost ten years, and they hadn't reached out.

He shrugged to himself. There was no accounting for people sometimes.

In the distance he heard hoof-beats and the rattle of trace chains. He stood, taking a final sip of his coffee before dropping a dime on the table. He looked around. Maude was still in the kitchen. "Stage is coming, Maude." He hollered loudly to warn her. There were usually a few passengers wanting some food and refreshment. He needed to get the letter on the stage and go find Thomas.

He grinned; Thomas was off gallivanting around with Sarah Mae Nunn again. Throughout all the problems they had faced with some of the townspeople this past year, Sarah Mae had stood by Thomas as a solid friend. Now, Thomas spent every minute he was in town with her.

He just hoped they wouldn't be too hard to find.

***** ******

"I wish I was the flower girl."

Thomas looked over at Sarah Mae. They were sitting on the porch in front of Maude's while he waited for Mr. William to get finished with his coffee.

She was staring off at the field where the late season flowers still bloomed brightly. "Why would you want to do that?"

Her head spun to face him, and he could see the hurt look on her face, "I mean…" He stammered, "I'm sure that dress will be all itchy. You'd be uncomfortable all-day long. You wouldn't want that, would you?"

Her face brightened at his concern, "Sure I would!"

Thomas shrugged, "I'd get out of it if I could. That collar itches something fierce." He sighed, "But, Mr. James asked me specifically to do it, and Mr. William says it's my 'duty to a friend.'" He offered a half-smile. Talking with Sarah Mae made him kind of uncomfortable. She always looked at him funny.

But even though she was a girl, she was his best friend. He figured all girls were like that, at least all the ones he knew. Miss Catherine always looked at Mr. James like that, and even Miss Maude looked at Mr. Earl that way.

Maybe girls had problems with their eyes?

Anyway, Sarah Mae had always stood by his side. Even when all the other kids wouldn't play with him, and for that, he was thankful. Even now, when most of the other kids had started acting normal again, he'd rather be with her.

As if reading his mind, Sarah Mae suddenly asked, "Why do you sit with me, instead of playing with the other kids?"

Thomas shrugged and thought a moment before he answered, "Well, back when the other kids wouldn't play with me, you always did."

"They play with you now."

He nodded, "I know, but..." He trailed off for a moment, "Well, Mr. James calls people like that persnickety."

She tilted her head, "What does that mean?"

"I'm not exactly sure, but I think..." He rubbed his cheek, "Well, Mr. William was showing me a verse in the Bible, how people who can't make up their mind to do right are unstable. I think it's like that. People who can't make up their mind. I'd rather be with someone who isn't persnickety."

Sarah Mae beamed at him, "You know so much about the Bible."

He swallowed hard. She was looking at him funny again. "Not as much as Mr. William does."

"Well, of course he does. He's the Parson. He has to. You don't have to."

Thomas thought for a moment, "Actually there's a verse in the Bible that tells us that we are all supposed to." He closed his eyes and quoted, "Study to shew thyself approved unto God." He opened his eyes and looked at her, "That was in one of Paul's letters to Timothy."

"Study? Like school?" She wrinkled her nose in disgust, "God wants us to do school?"

"No," Thomas shook his head, "I think that's just our Ma's. God wants us to study the Bible." He frowned, "Though, I guess you have to learn to read and such to do that."

"Yeah," Sarah Mae nodded sadly, "I suppose you do."

They both noticed the rattle of chains in the distance, and they both turned to look down the trail. "Stage is finally coming," Thomas offered quietly. It made him kind of sad because that meant it would be time to go soon.

The stage rode fast into town and pulled up in a flurry of dust that temporarily blocked their view of it. As the driver swung down, they heard the jingle of the bell that hung over the store's door and looked back as boots sounded on the boardwalk behind them. They stood quickly as the Sheriff limped down the walk from the store, grinning broadly at them.

"Hello, Mr. James." Thomas offered quietly. He liked Mr. James.

Mr. James grinned broadly, "Howdy, kids. You aren't getting into any trouble out here, are ya?"

"No, sir." Sarah Mae grinned back at the Sheriff, "We're just waiting for Parson William to finish up." She tilted her head, "Did you hurt your leg, Sheriff?"

James jerked his head back toward the store, "Miss Catherine dropped a pot on my foot." He winked at them, "But don't go saying anything."

"We won't, Sheriff..." Sarah Mae promised gravely. "Are you ready for the wedding?"

Mr. James puffed out his chest, "Sure am... matter of fact, I'm heading out to the house to do some more work. I want it to be perfect for Miss Catherine."

Sarah Mae smiled, "That's nice. I'm certain she will love it, Sheriff."

The passengers began piling out of the stage and moving toward the restaurant, and Mr. James moved to the side to make room for them to pass. As he moved, the door to Maude's swung open behind them, and Mr. William came out onto the boardwalk.

Mr. William nodded to Mr. James, then looked down at them, smiling, "Well, hello there. Looks like a party that I wasn't invited to. You two aren't causing the Sheriff trouble, are you?" He winked at Mr. James, and Thomas knew he was kidding.

"No, sir. We were just waiting for you."

"Ah, that's good." He held the door open as a few passengers went in and looked over at Mr. James, "James, coming from the store?" He pretended to sniff the air, "Must've... I smell love in the air today."

Mr. James laughed aloud, "Oh, Parson, let me tell you, it's not just me!"

Thomas lifted an eyebrow, somewhat confused since all he could smell was dust, but Mr. William just grinned and turned his attention to Sarah Mae. "Hello, Sarah Mae, how is your family doing?"

She smiled shyly, "They're doing fine, Parson William."

He nodded, "Tell them I said hello, would you?" The last passenger passed him, and he let the door shut, then looked over at Thomas, "You about ready to go, Thomas? I just need to give this to Ray, and we'll be ready."

"Yes, Sir." He looked over at Sarah Mae and tipped his hat, "Be seeing you, Sarah Mae."

She looked at him all funny again and smiled, "Goodbye, Thomas. See you Sunday."

Thomas nodded and followed Mr. William off the porch as they headed toward the stage, confused by the peals of laughter behind him coming from Mr. James.

***** ******

"Mr. William, can we stop back by the store?"

William looked over at Thomas. He had belted on his small pistol and was waiting for him to finish saddling the horse, "Sure, why?"

Thomas grinned, "Grandpa gave me a nickel. Told me to get some candy." His smile slowly relaxed, "Is it alright if I call him Grandpa?"

William had to admit, it was strange hearing someone call his Father Grandpa, but it didn't bother him, "Well, what does he say?"

Thomas shrugged, "He asked me to."

William recoiled in surprise, "Really?"

"Yes, Sir."

Confused, William rubbed his chin, "Why would you ask me, then?"

"I didn't want to offend you."

William chuckled softly, "You're not going to offend me, Thomas." He turned and pulled the saddle from his horse and sat it on the workbench.

"Even if I don't call you Pa?"

William turned and looked at Thomas. He was staring at the ground, not wanting to look up. At least now he had a small inkling about what was going on in the boy's head. "Look, Thomas, I know you loved your Pa, so no, it doesn't bother me that you want to keep his memory. I'm fine with Mr. William, or Parson on Sunday." He tousled the boy's hair, "Now let's go get you some candy." He wondered why the boy hadn't thought of getting candy when they were right in front of the store earlier, but he supposed Thomas's mind had been more on Sarah Mae than candy.

Maybe James was right.

Thomas had a wide grin plastered on his face as they led the horses quickly up the street toward the store. They tied the horses to the rail and had just made the boardwalk when the door to the store swung open. Becky Winters stepped out, followed by her son, Nathan, and finally her husband Andrew. They were one of the families that had been stirring up trouble for him ever since he'd been involved in a shooting a few weeks beforehand. They felt a parson had no business with a gun and were to the point of talking about starting another Church... in a town that six months ago didn't even have one.

William felt his pulse rate quicken in annoyance, but still forced a smile on his face. His Father had once told him that... *'Stress is the pressure put on your body when you have to force yourself to not slap someone who desperately needs it.'*

He was definitely feeling that urge at the moment, but he smiled anyway.

It was then that Becky noticed him and Thomas. She looked down her nose at him, "Mr. Stone..." and then her glance dropped to Thomas. "Oh, look. He has *you* wearing a gun as well. Expecting trouble, are we?"

William's jaw tightened, and he bit back a sharp retort, but Thomas spoke suddenly from next to him.

"Yes, Ma'am. Out here a body should always 'spect trouble."

She huffed and turned to go, but Thomas continued, "It's like Marshal Sterling told me, you've got to watch out for snakes, both the crawlers, and the two-legged kind."

Her head snapped around, "Well, I don't think there are any 'two-legged kind' in town."

Thomas stared at her wide eyed and persisted innocently, "Well, Ma'am, the Marshal said there was, and he got a good look at the town."

Her eyes widened, "Well, I never!" She brushed past them both with another loud huff, followed by her husband and son. As they passed, neither would meet William's eyes.

Holding back a small smile, William glanced down at Thomas, who was standing patiently waiting. He patted Thomas on the shoulder and nodded to the door, "Let's get that candy. I think you definitely deserve it right now."

***** ******

There were only two horses tied to the rail when they rode up and dismounted. Tom flipped his reins over the rail and looked across the street at the jail. "They got a jail, but no saloon?" He threw a questioning glance over at Miller.

Miller shrugged and dismounted, "Was the same last time too. Weren't no Sheriff neither."

"All the same, let's just get some grub and..." Tom trailed off as he looked around the town. "No hotel either?" He looked back at Miller again, "What kind of town is this?"

Miller shrugged, "We was just passing through."

Tom gestured to the store, "Well, go ask while I check the Sheriff's office." He crossed the street as the others stepped up onto the boardwalk and headed toward the store.

He glanced in the Sheriff's office but couldn't see anyone moving around inside. Sighing, he rapped his knuckles on the door, then opened it and peeked in. It was clean and neat, but definitely empty.

That was likely a good thing.

He crossed back over to the store and pulled open the door, pausing for a moment before walking in.

Wilfred was leaned over the counter, ogling the girl behind it. He was trying to talk sweet or something, but Tom could tell by the look on her face she was terrified.

"What's going on, boys?" Tom asked slowly.

Wilfred looked over and grinned, waving a book. "I was tryin' to talk to this purdy young thing, but she's too busy looking at this here book."

The girl behind the counter didn't look up; she was obviously frightened. Tom crossed the room in just a few steps and grabbed the book from Wilfred. He shook his head, "Knock it off, you fool." He slapped Wilfred's arm with the book and then dropped it back down on the counter. "My apologies, Ma'am." She looked up at that point, and Tom had to admit that Wilfred was right. She sure was pretty. Maybe they could talk to her for...

His train of thought was interrupted as Wilfred stepped back and dropped his hand to his gun. "Who do you think you are, Tom? You don't..."

"Is there a problem, gentlemen?"

Tom turned slowly at the low voice, a smile tugging at the corner of his mouth when he realized it was a Reverend standing a few feet from him. He opened his mouth to say something when his eyes dropped to the low-slung holster on the Reverend's waist. It was well worn and by the man's easy stance, he would guess that it was him that had worn it. Motion to his right showed a young boy hiding behind the end of the shelf with something in his hand. His eyes narrowed, was it a gun? He cut his eyes over to Wilfred who was still by the counter.

Wilfred had shifted and was grinning widely at the Reverend, "Well now, Reverend, I'll be the first to admit that I may have caused a little fuss here and there..."

The Reverend's eyes danced with amusement as he cut him off, "Make it there, not here."

Tom stepped forward and put his hand on Wilfred's shoulder. "Reverend, I was just about to suggest to my... compatriots that we leave."

"What?" Jefferies spoke suddenly from the other side of the room, "You're going to let him..." he trailed off as Miller hit his shoulder and nodded at the door.

"We're leaving," Miller agreed, then snorted a quiet laugh. "Yeah. It's a hard town that has a Reverend ready to shoot you. I'd hate to see what the lady behind the counter would do."

Tom pushed Wilfred toward the door, tipping his hat to the young woman behind the counter as he passed, "Ma'am... sorry to have bothered you." He walked straight out of the store and headed for his horse.

Wilfred started mouthing as soon as they stepped off the boardwalk, "Why'd you back down like that? Letting some sky-pilot shove you around."

Tom rounded on him, his face furious, "Look you twerp, that man would have ate you for breakfast. You better learn to be a better judge of men or you'll end up pushing daisies from the underside."

"Womenfolk too," Miller spoke sardonically as he swung into his saddle, "Little woman had a derringer palmed and hidden in the folds of her skirt. Soon as shootin' started, she would have nailed you." He offered with a chuckle, "And given that response, I wouldn't be too sure there wasn't a few more of 'em running around, ready to shoot."

Tom laughed as he mounted his horse, "There was a boy to the side of the Reverend. I think he was packing as well." He shook his head, "No, boys. We have enough problems without getting a bunch of trigger-happy townspeople after us. I think we'd better push up the road and find someplace else to stop for the night."

***** ******

Catherine took a slow sip of her tea. She was holding the cup tightly, trying to keep it from rattling on the saucer, "I don't know, Maggie. I just get so tired of feeling scared. When those men came in today..." She trailed off with a sigh before continuing. "I get so scared, but then I get mad because I'm scared. I just want to shoot someone."

Maggie chuckled softly, "Well, I guess you could go with that."

Catherine frowned, "No one would take it seriously. The only person I've ever shot asked me to marry him afterward."

They shared a quiet laugh as Catherine looked around the small restaurant. The only other people in the room were Mrs. Winters and her husband, who were sitting at the table nearest the window so Mrs. Winters could scoff at anyone who happened to pass by. She had met Doc Maggie here for a quiet cup of tea to calm her nerves after what happened in the store. Ted and Elizabeth were watching the store while she waited for James to get back.

She was tired of feeling scared, she was tired of living with fear every time someone came through the door. Honestly, what it boiled down to was that she was tired of working at the store. When she'd come west, she had thought it was going to be better than home and, in some ways, it was.

But then there were days like this. Ever since the robbery...

Maggie pursed her lips, "Well, something to consider is that the store seems to be the focal point of your stress. What are your plans after the wedding? Are you still going to work there?"

"Oh, I hope not." She took another sip of tea, "Once James finishes the house, I think we'll be fine with his salary."

Maggie smiled knowingly, "And you're ready for all the gardening and animal tending that comes with that?"

Catherine rolled her eyes, "I don't think anyone can really be ready for all that." She shook her head, "I mean, Ted has *let* me feed the chickens for the past few weeks, and that has been trying enough." Her brother in law had been extra cautious about certain jobs since the attempted robbery, but evidently felt that feeding chickens was safe.

Maggie laughed softly, "But, you're still willing?"

Catherine wrinkled her nose, "Well, that's what love is about, right? Doing things that you'd rather not do, simply because you love someone."

Maggie shrugged, "I'm not sure where chickens fit in with that, but yes."

They shared a quiet laugh and finished their tea. The door opened and Earl, James' brother, came in and nodded a quick greeting to them. "Ladies."

"Hi, Earl." As he passed, Catherine greeted the older man with a warm smile, "Is James back in town?"

Earl scratched his jaw, "No, Ma'am... I just needed to come check on some things. He's still out at the house."

Disappointed, she nodded, "Oh, alright."

Earl dipped his head and limped slowly across the room, taking a table in the corner. Catherine hid a smile and nudged Maggie's arm, motioning her to watch as Maude practically danced out of the kitchen to take his order—which was a feat for the sixtyish year-old woman.

She'd noticed that over the past few weeks, Earl had been spending more and more time at the restaurant.

"Are they sweet on each other?" Maggie whispered quietly.

"I think so," Catherine whispered back, "but I haven't decided if it's sweet or strange. They're so..." She trailed off with a wave of her hand.

"Old," Maggie finished. "You can say it. But..." She grinned wickedly, "Doesn't that make James old as well? Earl *is* his brother, not his father."

"Oh, stop. You're supposed to be making me feel better, Doctor." She leaned back in her chair, "Just because your beau is a younger man..."

Maggie blushed furiously, "He's not my beau... he's just, nice."

"Nice, eh?" Catherine chuckled, "I would say that..." she broke off as the door slammed open.

James barreled through looking frantically around the room, noticeably relieved when he spotted her. "Are you alright?" He demanded.

She could see the anger and concern on his face. She stood, trying to stave off the sudden rush of emotion that threatened to bring tears to her eyes. She didn't want to bawl like a baby, but seeing him so upset... "I'm fine." She finally sputtered. "It wasn't really anything, just some man who was..."

"Lucky I weren't here, is what he was." He cast a sour look at the door, "Can't believe the Parson didn't just shoot him."

"James!" She slapped his arm, "You can't talk like that." Her eyes flickered to Mrs. Winters, who had perked up at James' outburst. "You're the Sheriff." While she had to admit his protective nature made her feel better, there were others in the room that might not understand he was just blowing off steam—ones who were making enough trouble as it was. She gave him a soft smile, "I was just sitting here talking with Maggie about everything, and now I'm fine."

James looked over at Maggie and reddened, "Oh, Doc... I didn't see you there." He looked down at the floor in sudden discomfort, "I'm sorry, ladies, I didn't mean to interrupt you."

Maggie stood up, grinning broadly as she dug in her purse for a coin, "Oh that's no problem, Sheriff. I was just leaving anyway."

James backed up a step, "No, I can come back..."

Maggie dropped a dime onto the table "No, I need to go anyway," She touched Catherine's arm, "I'll stop by Elizabeth's house later, alright?"

"That's fine... and thanks." There was an uncomfortable silence as Maggie left the room. Catherine turned to James and smiled, "So, how was your day?"

James looked up and smiled hesitantly, "I didn't mean to run her off."

"Oh, James..." She sat back down at the table, and gestured to the other seat, "Have a seat. It was fine so stop worrying about it. She was just keeping me company until you arrived anyway. And as far as the thing in the store earlier today, it wasn't your fault. I wasn't hurt, I just panicked." She patted his arm as he sat, "Now, how did it go at the house today? Did you get much done?"

James frowned at the change of topic and cast an annoyed glance toward the door, "No... Well, some. I was just starting on the chimney when the Parson rode up and told me what happened."

"I'm sorry that you had to stop."

"No... I didn't mind, I was just worried about you." He finally noticed his brother in the corner, "Wha...?" He stood again, his face contorted somewhere between annoyance and laughter, "Earl, you old coot!" He hollered across the restaurant, causing Mrs. Winters to jump sharply. "I thought you had to go take a nap, 'cause you were 'tired.'"

Earl grinned sheepishly, holding up a cup like a shield. "Needed a cup of coffee before I lay down."

"Harrumph." James sat back in his chair and faced Catherine. "Codger left a bit before Parson rode up, said he was tuckered out and needed a nap." He waved at Maude, who had finally come out of the kitchen, and signaled her for a cup of coffee. "No wonder he can't get any work done. He's busy drinking coffee."

Catherine sat back in her chair and smiled. If James hadn't realized why his brother was constantly at the restaurant, she wasn't going to tell him.

***** ******

Interlude

Northwest Colorado

Sheriff Jesse Molvin squinted into the setting sun and held up his fist. "Ho, there." The group of riders slowed to a stop behind him.

"What do you see, Jesse?"

"Smoke." The Sheriff pointed to a thin trail on the horizon before turning back to the Doc. "Probably where those Utes came from."

Doc Gentry lifted himself up in his stirrups to get a better look, "Anyone live out that way?"

"Nah, probably some travelers got caught out." Dave Riggens offered, then spat to the side of his horse. He had a sour look on his face. His right arm was roughly bandaged and hanging loosely at his side—he'd taken a bullet when the Ute war-party attacked—it was only a flesh wound, but a stark reminder of the danger they might face if they continued going forward. "We ought to check though."

Sheriff Molvin looked around, "Yeh, just be ready. It'll be getting dark soon, and those Utes will still be out."

Dave chuckled, the sound contrary to the look on his face, "Only one got away, and he'll be done for soon enough... 'sides, we need to see if'n the kid made it that far."

Sheriff Molvin nodded slowly and looked back at the rest of the men. Farmers, townspeople, and even the blacksmith had volunteered to come out to catch the kid; solid men whose entire savings were reflected in that bag the kid got away with. He and his gang had timed their robbery well, getting in right as one of the local ranchers had brought a deposit from a sale.

Of course, that was the only timing that had went well for them, considering the undertaker was laying the other three out for burying. Either way, they needed to catch this last one, and get the money back for the town. He blew out a breath and flicked the reins, pushing his horse forward.

Part of him was still cursing his own stupidity. He could've shot the kid—had him dead in his sights all the way out of town—but, as he watched the red-plaid shirt get further away, he couldn't pull the trigger. He knew the kid had dropped his gun in the bank and couldn't see shooting an unarmed man in the back... even if he was stealing a few thousand in gold.

But now they were miles from town, and with the added stress of getting attacked by that band of Utes... He shot a quick glance back at the line of men following him. If one of the men had died when the Ute's attacked, it would've been his fault...

Sheriff Molvin shook the thought off and spurred his horse forward.

Even riding cautiously, it took less than twenty minutes before they spotted the source of the smoke.

"Lord have mercy..." Zeke muttered as they topped out the hill that overlooked the burned-out wagon train. From their position, they could see bodies littering the ground—a sharp contrast to the spring flowers that dotted the hillside like a bright purple blanket.

They pulled up, carefully surveying the carnage from a distance.

"Anyone see anything moving down there?"

There was silence while all eyes focused on the carnage below.

"Movement!" Dave spoke sharply as he twisted on his horse and lifted his Spencer rifle to his shoulder.

Sheriff Molvin looked over, "You sure it's one of them Utes, Dave?"

A shot rang out from the bottom the hill, followed immediately by the dull roar of Dave's Spencer rifle.

Dave lowered his Spencer, "Yup. Purty sure."

The Sheriff nodded as Dave spit to the side again. "Good shot."

They rode down the hill slowly, rifles ready in case there were any other hostiles. As they reached the bottom, they split into two separate groups and moved carefully through the wagons searching for survivors.

Sheriff Molvin had just stopped near one of the wagons when Zeke called from the other side.

"Hey, Sheriff! Look here!"

The Sheriff looked over... Zeke was standing over a dead horse. He lifted himself up in his stirrups to see better, "Whatcha got?"

"The robber's horse... and the gold."

"Sheriff, over here!" Doc Gentry called out about a dozen feet from Zeke, close to a burned-out wagon. "I found the robber!"

The Sheriff nudged his horse, moving over to the body... slowing as he passed the wagon. On the ground, face up, was a young man in a plaid shirt. He'd been shot several times and was obviously dead. His eyes flickered to the empty holster on the young man's side. "That him?"

Doc Gentry looked up with a grin, "Yep. That's the robber. He didn't get far, did he?"

"Harumph!" Zeke coughed, "I bet that Ute got him." He hooked a thumb toward Dave, "The one Dave got... kid must've rode in and got kilt by the Ute."

Sheriff Molvin nodded slowly as he looked at the sky, "I reckon... we'd better get moving then. We need to get these bodies buried and head back to town."

***** ******

Sheriff Molvin's eyes narrowed in the failing light as he watched the others dig graves for the fallen settlers.

They were taking too much time; even though they had beaten off the Ute war party, they didn't know if there were any more out there lurking around and waiting for a chance to pick them off. He wanted to get home as quickly as they could, but they couldn't leave the settlers bodies for the vermin.

He cut his gaze up to Dave, who was perched on top of the hill watching carefully for movement. Dave was a good shot, but once the sun was gone, he'd be useless up there.

He stroked his chin and looked to the south. He hadn't said anything to the others, but he'd walked around the area, checking the area... and had noticed there had been several survivors of the raid.

He'd first noticed it on the far side, tracks where a man in riding boots had led a horse down and through the small wash, heading south. Following the tracks backward had led him to a small wagon.

Three sets of tracks. A man, a woman, and a child... the woman and child had mounted the horse, and the man led them out of the area. He'd tracked him backwards from the wagon the woman and child had emerged from, around the area and straight back over to the dead appaloosa.

He had no doubt that it was the kid from the bank; a quick glance at the feet of the dead man in the plaid shirt the others *thought* was the robber confirmed his suspicions. The dead man was wearing sturdy work-boots, not riding boots like the kid had worn...

But the man that led out the horse with the woman and child was wearing those same narrow heeled riding boots.

He spat to the side. There was no way he was going to give chase. If there were more Indians out there, they were all in trouble.

But even if not, as far as the others knew the kid was dead. He'd left the gold behind, so there was no reason to even think about changing the narrative. Besides, he knew the kid wasn't a killer. Leaving the gold and choosing to protect a woman and a child had proved it. This might give that kid a chance to stay on the good path.

Of course, if the kid was intent on a life of robbing banks, fate would eventually catch up with him. But he wasn't going to risk these men to find out.

He turned slowly and walked back to the group of graves they had dug.

***** ******

THREE

Nate stopped the horse and looked around. The three-quarters moon was almost directly overhead and was casting a harsh glare on the grassy terrain.

"Is everything alright?" The woman's voice contained undisguised fear. It was the first she had spoken for hours—really, it was the first words she'd spoken since leaving the wagon train.

"Yes'm. Just thirsty." He stepped over, patting the horse on the side of his muzzle as he grabbed his canteen from the saddle horn and took a long drink. He could hear frogs in the distance and was pretty sure they were near a creek. He took a final pull from his canteen and offered it to the woman... He vaguely remembered her name was Mary. "We'll need to make camp pretty soon." Nate gestured to the little girl—he still couldn't remember her name—as she huddled in Mary's arms. "Little girl looks about done in."

Mary accepted the canteen, staring at it for a few moments before hanging it back on the saddle horn. "Nate?" Despite the moon, he still couldn't make out her facial expression, but could clearly hear the exhaustion in her voice. "Can we stop now? For at least a little rest?"

Nate tightened his jaw—He should have realized they would need a break. "Yes'm..." He gestured to a line of trees visible in the moonlight a few hundred yards to their left. "I think there'll be a spot over there. Sounds like water, and there's some trees for cover."

"I..." she trailed off, looking uncomfortable, "Well, how long until we reach a town?"

He twisted his mouth in thought, "Well, Ma'am... I don't rightly know. I never rode this way 'til now."

"So, we'll have to stay out here? Without shelter?"

He nodded slowly, "Yes'm. Sorry 'bout that, but..." He shrugged, "I don't know how far away the Ute's are, but I know they are in that direction," he hooked his thumb the way they had come from, "So I want to keep heading the other way. Only way to be certain to miss them." He started pulling the horse toward the tree line. He was glad that he'd thought to grab a few blankets—it was cool out, and they couldn't chance a fire right now. It would be a beacon to draw in the enemy... which at this point was pretty well anybody.

He stopped just inside the tree line and tied the reins to a low branch. "Ma'am, let me help you down." He reached out for the little girl, picking her easily from the back of the horse. She made no sound, but immediately snuggled against his chest.

Mary had clambered down from the horse and moved over to him, holding out her arms, "Clara, come to me." Though exhausted, her voice carried an edge. He assumed it was leftover fear from the slaughter at the wagon train.

Nate passed the sleeping girl over to her mother and started pulling the bedrolls from the horse. "You take these and make up a bed for you and your daughter, and I'll take care of the horse." He could hear the bubbling of a nearby creek and wanted to water the horse and refill his canteen before settling in.

Mary nodded simply, accepting the blankets and moving off to a small patch of ground barely visible through the filtered moonlight.

Nate watched her as she started spreading out the blankets, and then quickly unsaddled the horse, rubbing it down with some dry leaves before leading it through the woods toward the creek. It didn't take long to find—the shimmering of moonlight from the surface of the water was easy to spot—and he filled the canteen while the horse drank. When it was finished, he led it back to the clearing and tied it close to a clump of grass so it could eat.

Now that he was finished with the horse, he was ready to settle down. He carried the saddle over and dropped it on the ground a few feet from the woman. She had already made a bed for the little girl and was sitting on the blanket next to her, wrapped in another blanket. She looked up, "Are you going to make a fire?" Her voice shook slightly from the cool night air.

"No Ma'am... I don't want to chance it. We don't know where the Ute's are." He dropped down to the ground, exhausted. The night *was* cool, but for now he was still warm from the movement—which was lucky, since he didn't have a third bedroll.

He looked around the clearing. With everything that had happened today, followed by the last twenty miles or more of walking, he was done in... but he knew he wouldn't be able to sleep. He needed to stay awake and keep watch. He leaned back against the saddle and pulled off his boots. His feet were killing him. It was obvious that riding boots weren't good for walking overland. He rubbed his feet gingerly, wishing that he had some nice slippers and his mom's liniment oil. That would feel nice.

He huffed out a quiet laugh—if he wasn't so tired, he'd have considered going down to the creek to soak his feet in the cold water.

"Are we safe?" Mary's soft voice barely carried across the space between them. He was certain that she was as exhausted as he was.

"Yes... yes, I think so." He pulled his boots back on and leaned back against the saddle. "We haven't seen any sign of being followed, and even if they were looking, they couldn't track us in the dark. I'd say we're good for now."

"Are you going to stay awake?"

He nodded slowly, then remembered she probably couldn't see him, "Yes, Ma'am. I'll be watching."

"Ok." She lay over next to her daughter. There was a long silence, interrupted only by the frogs in the trees. Finally, he heard her quiet voice, "Thank you, Nate."

Nate nodded silently, the words he wanted to offer had stuck in his throat as a burst of emotion almost overwhelmed him. It had been a horrible, horrible day. When he'd woken up that morning, he hadn't imagined that by the end of the day he would have seen three men gunned down, be running for his life from an armed posse, and almost get killed by a couple of renegade Utes.

And never in his life would he have guessed that instead of running to save his own life, he would be risking his to save a woman and her child.

He blew out a long breath and shifted against the saddle. He knew that by himself he could have been miles further away, but now he was stuck and was probably going to get caught and hung, trying to keep them safe. He had tried, unsuccessfully, throughout the day to work himself up and be angry over the situation, but in the end, he could feel nothing but shame. They didn't ask for him to rob a bank. They were just crossing the prairie, probably with the idea that they were on the way to a better life, and all the sudden they lost everything and everyone *they* knew—

including the girl's father who was probably one of those men that he had left unburied back at the wagon train. They'd been through worse than anything that he'd been through—worse, since his was self-inflicted—and that was the source of shame had been surging through him all through the day.

And now, despite all her losses, here she was thanking him. He didn't deserve a thank you. He deserved a noose and admitting that to himself had been like getting hit with a hammer. He was simply so overwhelmed that he couldn't even speak.

Finally, after what seemed like an eternity, he was able to whisper, "No problem."

But she was already asleep.

***** ******

Nate woke up with a start, but he didn't move—he lay in place, listening intently to the night sounds. He hadn't meant to fall asleep; he'd just been so tired... but something had woken him, and he wasn't certain what it had been.

He reached out slowly and grasped the butt of his pistol, glad that he'd had it within reach, and lifted his head looking around the camp. Mary was sleeping soundly, wrapped up in one of the blankets a few feet away, and Clara...

With a start, he realized the little girl was gone.

He sat up slowly and looked around the small camp, finally spotting her in the flickering moonlight on the far edge of the clearing, staring into the woods.

Nate slipped quietly from his spot on the ground, creeping across to where the little girl was standing, curious what she was watching—hoping it wasn't an Indian... or worse, the posse.

As he neared, the little girl turned slowly, her finger over her lips in a shushing gesture, and then pointed into the trees.

Nate looked, smiling at the sight of a small deer feeding, maybe forty feet away. He grinned, noting that the wind was at his face which was why the deer hadn't smelled them. He looked down at Clara who had turned back and was watching the deer with unabashed interest. He slowly holstered his pistol, dropping to a crouch and watched with her until the deer moved off slowly into the trees.

As it disappeared, Nate leaned over slightly and whispered, "Pretty neat, eh, Clara?"

She turned and beamed, her smile showing a neat row of white teeth.

He was amazed how resilient the young girl was. Despite everything that had happened she was still able to smile. "Have you ever seen a deer that close?"

Clara twisted her mouth, looking off to the side as she thought, then shook her head.

Nate grinned, "Well, I'm glad you got to see that one... maybe we'll get to see something else fun... like a skunk."

Clara giggled and pinched her nose.

Chuckling, he gestured back to the camp, "We'd best get back, before your Ma wakes up."

She sighed audibly, and nodded, holding out her hand. He hesitated for a moment before taking her hand; it was cold and fragile feeling. He held it gently, like a robin's egg, afraid it would break as they walked back to the camp.

He didn't know much about little girls, but Johnny Bode had a little sister who was always tagging after him, and she always had an old rag-doll clutched in her hand. He realized that was what was missing. "Don't you have a doll, or somethin'?" He glanced down at her to make sure he wasn't moving faster than her little legs could and smiled at the look of concentration on her face. Finally, the little girl shook her head demurely and looked back down at her feet.

"Oh, sorry. Did it get left at the wagon?"

She looked up at him and nodded curtly. In the moonlight he could see one corner of her mouth turned down, giving her face a comical, lopsided look.

"That's a bummer. Well, wait..." He stopped and pulled a half-whittled figure of a bear from his pocket. He stunk at whittling, and it didn't look much like a bear, but it was the best he could do. "Would you like this bear? It's not very good..." He trailed off, holding it out to see if she wanted it.

She snatched it from his hand with a grin, holding it up in the moonlight to get a look before clutching it to her chest.

His smiled for a moment, but his face fell quickly when he remembered that she'd lost her Pa that morning. A wooden bear wasn't much compensation. He lowered his voice, "Sorry 'bout everything that happened today. It's not easy to lose your Pa."

Clara tilted her head to the side with a questioning look.

Nate felt a stab of pity—he guessed she didn't know her Pa had died yet—and he certainly didn't want to be the one to inform her. He shrugged apologetically and looked down at the girl's Ma. She was still sleeping soundly, oblivious to the little girl being up. He looked at the moon, finding it lower in the sky, "Only a few hours left to rest, then we'll be moving again." He thought for a moment, "Well, Clara, I s'pose you best get in bed."

The little girl grinned and flopped down on the blanket her mother had laid out, immediately wrapping the other around her like a cocoon so only her face was visible, shining white in the moonlight,

He smiled at her antics; amazed at her resilience. "Get to sleep now."

She nodded, clutched the wood figure to her chest, and closed her eyes.

He watched her for a long moment, his eye flickering to her sleeping mother before turning and walking back over to his spot by the saddle. He sat there for a long time, watching their sleeping forms, wondering what the woman was going to do once they got to a town.

***** ******

The sun was barely peering over the horizon when Nate saddled the horse. He was ready to go, but was waiting for the woman and her daughter to finish washing up. Drumming his fingers on the saddle to pass the time, he looked cautiously around, half expecting to see the posse moving toward him. He half hoped they had given up after the Ute's attacked, but knew he couldn't count on it. He had no choice but to keep riding in the opposite direction; at least until he could find a place for Mary and her daughter. He squatted down and picked up a small stick, using it to trace a rough map on the ground. He, Jed, Simmons, and Hank had come south from Bitter Creek, Wyoming, crossing the mountains and heading almost due south before running into Klein. After leaving Klein, he'd ridden almost due east before coming across the wagon train—maybe twenty miles? After that, they had been slowly moving northeast... it seemed like they should be getting close to the Bear River. He figured he'd cross that, leading them up past the Little Snake River into southern Wyoming... possibly hooking up with the railroad.

He frowned and sat back on his heels. No, he'd have to plan carefully where they met the railroad. He'd hooked up with Jed and his friends in Washakie before heading further west—the people there may recognize him and start asking questions. No... he drug the stick to the right, creating a longer line... they'd have to go further east. He closed his eyes, trying to remember the towns that were further east. Separation was one he remembered—interesting name, and much further east than he'd been when he'd met Jed and the others.

"Are you ready, Nate?"

Nate looked over; Mary and her daughter were coming up from the creek, their faces bright from scrubbing with the cold water. "Yes, Ma'am. I was just trying to plan which way to go."

"Will we reach a town today?" Her face was hopeful, and he hated to say no.

"Well, Ma'am, I hope so." He nodded toward the small horse, "Not really certain how far we are from a town, and with one horse 'twixt us, we're moving slow." He wanted to whine about how bad his feet hurt already after walking all day yesterday, but he didn't want her to feel like he regretted taking them with him.

Her brow furrowed, but she nodded slowly, "I understand."

"Here." He held out some beef jerky—the sum total of the food he had grabbed from the wagon train... well, that and the three bags he'd thought was food, but turned out to be tea. "Y'all nibble on this. It's all we got for now, but I don't want to go hunting yet."

"Thank you." Mary accepted the jerky from him and handed one of the pieces to Clara, motioning for her to eat it.

He held the horse as Mary climbed awkwardly into the saddle, then handed Clara up to her. Once she and her daughter were settled, he led the horse out of the trees toward the northeast, and by the time the sun was fully over the horizon they could no longer see the wooded area they had camped in.

***** ******

Mary held tightly onto her sister as Nate led the horse down a long hill toward a stretch of tall trees. He hadn't said much to her since they left camp, despite her efforts to talk. The most she had gotten from him was the speculation that they might come across a town, and that he'd leave her and Clara there.

She had mixed feeling about that. Part of her was looking forward to continuing their journey west to California, but the other part didn't want to separate from Nate, whose presence had made her feel safe for the first time in a while.

She'd been watching him carefully throughout the day. He hadn't been very talkative about his past. She wasn't an expert but based on his reticence she was pretty certain he'd done something he was ashamed of.

But she was just as certain it wasn't *bad*.

Of course, she barely knew him, but he had already been such a blessing. He had not only rescued them from the wagon but had walked all day and stayed up all night just to keep them safe. She felt like she could trust him, and that wasn't something she offered easily. She had met a lot of men over the past few months that had claimed to be trustworthy—and she had known for a fact that none of them were. She smiled grimly at the memory of several men that often came into the laundry that she would have been more scared of than the Indians, but Nate was... different.

She looked down at Clara. The little girl was dozing fitfully as she clutched the carved pinecone Nate had given her—she supposed it had been at some point in the night while she slept—and Clara hadn't let loose of it yet. *That* was saying something for a little girl that often misplaced things. The more she thought about it, the more she realized that part of the reason she trusted Nate was Clara's attitude toward him. The little girl had shown a sixth sense toward men, immediately letting her know when there was one she should avoid, and she overwhelmingly seemed to like Nate. That told her that even if he had done something, he was still a good person.

And honestly, that gave her hope about herself. If he could still be good, maybe she could too.

"Ma'am? You alright?"

Startled from her reverie, she looked down. Nate was still leading the horse toward the tree line. "Yes, Nate... I'm fine."

"Gonna stop for a bit, fill up the canteen." He gestured to the trees, "There's a creek running through there."

"Ok." She nudged Clara awake as they passed into the grove of trees. He stopped the horse a few feet in, looping the reins on a low branch. Shifting, Mary handed Clara down to Nate before allowing him to help her from the horse.

Nate sat heavily on the ground and leaned back against a small tree. "You two go ahead and clean up. I'm going to rest for a few."

She hated for Nate to keep putting himself out for them, but was quite happy to get off the horse for a while. She walked gingerly down to the creek, carefully stepping on rocks to avoid getting her feet wet.

After washing up and drinking deeply from the small creek, Mary sat down by a tree across from Nate while Clara wandered between the trees.

"Sweet girl." Nate offered suddenly, "What is she, four?"

"Yes, just turned." She chuckled softly, "And you think she's sweet, until you ask her to finish her potatoes." She looked over; Clara was pulling at a flower with one hand—the other was clutching the carved pinecone. "Nate, I appreciate everything you've done for us." She thought for a moment, "And it was really sweet to give Clara that pinecone. She hasn't let loose of it all day."

Nate shifted slightly and leaned forward, "Pinecone? I didn't..." He looked over at Clara and his face suddenly went red. "Oh, that... no problem."

Mary's eyes narrowed as she watched his reaction. Something was... "Wait, was that a pinecone?"

He shrugged, waving his hand dismissively, "Wasn't supposed to be, but I reckon it does kind of look like one." He shifted awkwardly, "My Pa was always good at whittlin'. I s'pose I'm not."

"No... it looks good." She felt bad for him, and hurried to change the subject, "So, have you always lived out..." She gestured awkwardly to their surroundings, "Here?"

"No Ma'am. Only been out west for a few months." His face softened, "Been meaning to ask you," He gestured to Clara, "Little girl... does she know her Pa's... well, gone?"

Mary felt her jaw tighten, "What do you mean?"

Nate looked down at his lap, "Not tryin' to pry, Ma'am. Just didn't know if she knew her Pa'd been..." He looked up awkwardly, "With the Ute's."

She blinked several times before realizing what he was saying, "Oh... no. Her father died last year. He wasn't on the wagon with us."

"Oh, sorry." He looked down awkwardly, obviously embarrassed.

"It's ok." She offered quietly. He finally looked up, and she noticed how red-rimmed his eyes were. "You look awful tired. Do you need to rest for a bit? I can keep watch." She watched him closely as he thought about it.

After a few seconds his jaw tightened, and he shook his head. "Not right now. I want to make sure we're safe."

"I can see if anyone is coming. I promise I'll wake you up." She thought for a moment, "It'll give Clara a little time to stretch her legs."

He finally nodded, "Alright, but just for a bit."

Mary smiled inwardly, hiding her satisfaction from him as he pulled his hat down over his eyes. It was only a few seconds before his breathing evened out, and she knew he was asleep.

She turned her head to watch Clara wander around the area. She was worried about her sister. She hadn't spoken since Horace and that was already a concern, but now with the attack on the wagon... even though she had tried to shield her from seeing the bodies, there was no way she could have missed all the gunfire and screams of horror and pain. The Indians had been searching wagon to wagon, killing those they found, and it would have only been a matter of minutes until her and her sister were found.

But then Nate arrived.

She cut her eyes over to where Nate was propped against the small tree but looked away immediately. She didn't want to be caught gawping at him if he woke up.

She forced her thoughts to her more immediate problem; if her and Clara showed up as the last survivors of the wagon train, it might start questions— questions she wouldn't want to answer. Perhaps some of the other passengers had relatives in Philadelphia? What if they sent investigators to discuss the massacre? What if they recognized her?

No, that would be a huge problem... and right then, she had no idea what she was going to do about it.

***** ******

FOUR

They traveled several more miles before the sun began slowly dipping down to the west. Nate knew they needed to find a place to camp, so he started looking for a safe place to stop for the night. There were still a few hours of daylight left, but despite the brief nap he had taken earlier in the day, he was beat.

Part of it was hunger; he hadn't grabbed much food when they left the wagons, and they had eaten it that morning. Of course, it wasn't just him he was worried about. He cast a backwards glance toward Mary and her daughter to check on them, but lost his footing and stumbled on the uneven ground.

"Are you alright?" Mary called out from behind him. "Do you need to ride for a while? I could walk."

"No, I'm fine..." Nate felt his face burn with embarrassment and continued walking without looking back. The last thing he wanted was for a woman to see him trip over his own feet like a kid.

They topped out a low hill, and he scanned the horizon, spotting a wooded area to the southeast. Even though it was a little out of their line of travel, he immediately started toward it. It would make a good place to make a shelter and get some rest.

They had barely crossed into the trees when Mary groaned loudly, "I was *so* ready to stop!" She announced with a laugh.

He grinned in response as he helped Clara down from the horse and then offered his hand to help Mary.

There was a small stream nearby for water, and Mary immediately walked Clara down while Nate dropped the bedrolls and saddlebags so they could set up camp. He left the horse saddled and waiting, and as soon as Mary returned, he rode out to hunt. They needed food, and he was hoping that by now they were far enough away from the Ute's to be safe—he just hoped to get something quickly.

Unfortunately, it took a while to find something suitable. He was a decent enough shot at short range, but he just wasn't as confident with long shots. Given that he only wanted to shoot once so the Indians couldn't track them, he was looking for something he could get close to. He passed on the squirrels he came across deciding that they were too small. After that he passed up a large mule deer—he knew that even if he did bring it down, there would be too much meat to carry or eat, and he didn't want to leave meat to waste and draw wolves.

He finally spotted a turkey and took it down easily with a single shot. He hoped it would provide them enough meat for a few meals. As he rode quickly back to the camp the sun was lighting up the grass with a burning orange glow as it started to touch the horizon. He watered the horse; unsaddling it and tying it to a tree before finally starting on the turkey.

Clara watched wide eyed as he plucked the large bird at the edge of camp.

"She's never seen a turkey up close before," Mary offered as she walked up. "Well, not with feathers still on it anyway."

"Really?" Nate cocked his head to the side and looked comically at Clara. "I figgered she'd be an old hand at this." He held the bird out, "You want to try?"

Clara shook her head and backed up a few steps, eliciting a soft chuckle from Mary. As Nate continued plucking, Clara edged forward and reached out tentatively for the tail-feathers.

Nate grinned and offered gently, "Go ahead, Clara... it won't hurt you."

She grabbed a handful and pulled, but none of the feathers came loose—which seemed to annoy her—so, she stuck her tongue out the side of her mouth and pulled again. This time her hand slipped loose, and she fell onto her backside.

"Whoa there!" Nate laughed aloud, offering his free hand to the small girl. "Need a hand up?"

Clara eyed his hand warily as if debating whether to trust him before reaching up and taking it. Once she made her feet, she moved in close and grabbed the feathers again. This time she gripped hard and gave them a great yank, finally succeeding in pulling a handful of feathers from the bird.

"There ya go!" Nate laughed aloud as the little girl held up the feathers triumphantly.

"That's good, Clara." Mary, still smiling, patted the girl on the shoulder, "But let's allow Nate to finish up while we get the camp ready."

Nate nodded, his eyes cutting to the west. The sun had dropped below the horizon and it was starting to get darker. "Well, I guess your Ma's right. Best let me finish up."

Clara nodded simply and turned back toward the camp, still clutching the feathers in her fist as she walked back with her Ma. Nate watched them retreat, then shook his head and continued working on the turkey.

***** ******

Mary cleaned up after supper, scrubbing the pan out with sand from the creek while Clara watched. Nate had retreated out to the edge of camp again and was working at a small piece of wood with his knife.

Mary tried to focus on getting the pan clean, but her eyes were drawn to Nate's profile in the flickering light.

"Choo!"

Surprised, Mary turned at the tiny voice. It was the first noise she had heard Clara make in the last several months. The little girl was wiping her nose.

"Are you alright, Clara?"

Clara nodded slowly, then paused—exploding with another small sneeze. *"Choo!"*

Mary frowned and reached out with the back of her hand to feel Clara's forehead. "Well, you don't feel warm, that's a relief." She blew out a frustrated breath. The cold nights with no shelter and the damp mornings had taken their toll on the little girl. She missed the security and warmth of the wagon.

But at least they were alive. She tousled Clara's hair, "Well, you'll probably feel better after a good night's rest. Let's get you ready for bed."

It didn't take long for Clara to wash her face and get tucked into the bedroll. Mary tucked her blanket around the little girl as well, snuggling her up tightly. By that time, Nate had moved back in closer to the fire. She finished packing the pan away and sat down on the edge of Clara's blanket, staring at the bright orange flames of the fire.

She had been numb with grief when Nate had first rescued them from the wagon train, and that feeling had moved to thankfulness and joy in their survival. But now, the longer they were out here, the more time she had to think about everything, the less joy she found. Her thoughts constantly dwelled on loss—how she had lost everything she had worked for, how she was going to have to start all over again, working and saving, in the hopes they could make a living out west, how she and her sister were still in constant danger even now. To top all of that off, she had let her sister get sick. It was all pressing down on her, proof she was a horrible person destined for failure. Proof that she should have...

The fire popped, and Mary jumped as a shower of sparks shot into the air.

Nate chuckled from his spot, "Sorry 'bout that, Ma'am. Reckon it's time to put the fire out."

Swallowing hard to remove the lump in her throat, Mary shook her head, "Nate... can we just leave the fire for a little while? Please?"

There was a long pause before he answered, "Yes'm. I can put it out later."

"Thank you." She breathed a sigh of relief. It wasn't that she was scared of the dark, it was that the memories were worse at night. She knew she should probably just climb into the bedroll with Clara, but something was drawing her to the flames, and she didn't want to leave.

***** ******

Nate sat back a little way from the small fire, staring out into the darkness. Mary had been sitting quietly near the fire since she'd tucked Clara into the bedroll. He'd thought about saying something to her but had no clue what to say. He'd never been very good at talking to womenfolk, and under their present circumstances he knew that it would be even harder to start a pleasant conversation. *'Nice weather we're having, ain't it? Not too hot or cold out. I guess the Indians picked a good time of year to kill everyone in your wagon train and put you on the run? Didn't they?'*

He shook his head. What he wanted to do was put out the fire and get some sleep, but he couldn't since it was an obvious comfort to Mary... more than any conversation with him would be.

Hoo! Hoo! An owl questioned somewhere in the darkness behind them. Nate grimaced at the question the owl posed—Who? Who was he? Who did he really want to be?

"Nate?" Mary's soft voice drug him from his thoughts.

"Yes'm." He answered without looking.

"Does everyone who kills somebody go to Hell?"

Nate shifted uncomfortably and glanced over at her. She was huddled close to the fire, trying to stave off the chill of the evening as she stared into the flickering flames. "Well, no... I don't think so." He rubbed his eye with the back of his thumb, "I mean, it's been a while since I've been to Church, but it seemed like there was a whole lotta killin' in the Bible—even the good guys—and they didn't go to Hell."

There was a thick silence for several moments, punctuated only by the hooting owl.

"How do you know if you're a good guy?"

He thought for a few moments, "Well, I reckon it depends on whether the people you killed needed killin'." He blew out a long breath, "It's like the Utes back there. They killed those settlers and that was murder... But the people defending themselves, those people... I'd say they were good."

"So, it's only good to kill someone trying to kill you?"

Nate paused for a moment, looking down at his lap, "I guess there are other reasons to kill someone..." He trailed off, uncomfortable about the line of questioning. He'd had to kill that Ute back at the train, but he didn't feel good about it.

Mary fell silent for several minutes, then asked, "Did you kill those Indians back there?"

Nate felt a cold knot in his stomach, "Yeh... one of them anyway. I left the other one trussed up by a wagon." He turned to face her and noticed the glittering of fresh tears on her cheeks as she watched him. "I, uh... I couldn't kill the other one... it seemed wrong." At her lifted eyebrow, he added... "I'd knocked him unconscious, and he was just lying there."

She nodded slowly, "Was that the only man you've killed? I mean..." She looked down at her lap, "I feel like you're hiding something..."

Nate shook his head, "No, Ma'am... I'd never killed anyone before... well, before this..." He swallowed with difficulty. His throat was tight, but he suddenly felt the urge to explain to her, "...but, that's not the only bad you can do. I'd hooked up with some... I guess they were just bad characters. They talked me into helping them rob a bank."

Mary looked up sharply, "You robbed a bank?" Her eyes narrowed, "Where's the money?"

Nate shook his head, "I left it back at the wagon train. I wanted no part of it anymore."

"Won't your friends come looking for it?"

Nate rubbed his chin, "They weren't really friends, but no, all three of them was killed. I'm the only one that got away."

They sat in an uncomfortable silence for several minutes as the fire crackled and the owl continued to question him. Finally, Mary offered quietly, "I killed a man."

Nate looked over—his eyes automatically tracking to the knife she kept by her side. "Really?" He didn't exactly know what to say at that point. "Uh, was it one of the Indians?"

She was still looking down at her lap, "No, he was my husband."

Nate edged slightly away from her, his hand reaching down to touch his pistol for reassurance. As his fingers touched the cold metal his eyes cut over to Clara, wrapped snugly in the only three blankets they possessed—how could a woman who would give up her blanket for a little girl and lie out in the cold be a cold-blooded killer? He shook his head, no—she wasn't a cold-blooded killer. There had to be more to it.

Unfortunately, there had been plenty of times in his life that he'd had difficulty finding the right words to say to someone... and right then seemed to be one of them. He was speechless. Swallowing hard, he tried to think of something comforting to say. "Um, really? Was there a... reason?" He looked back over; she was crying, her shoulders heaving with silent sobs. His jaw tightened, and he tried again. "I mean, I'm sure he needed killin'."

Her voice, barely audible, sounded tortured, "He wouldn't stop." She looked up, "He was beating Sarah, and wouldn't stop."

Nate blinked a few times in confusion before he understood. The little girl—Clara wasn't her real name. "Is that why she won't talk?"

Mary nodded slowly, "Yes. I couldn't let him keep hurting her."

Horrified that some man would be able to attack a sweet girl like Clara, Nate shook his head slowly and cleared his throat before responding, "Well, Ma'am... I'll be honest with you. I don't consider myself a killer, but I don't think that I would have hesitated to stop a man from beating a little girl, even if it were his own. I don't blame you."

Mary looked up, her voice quavering with emotion, "Sarah wasn't his. She's my sister."

"Oh." His eyes dropped to the sleeping figure, "She was living with you?"

Mary sighed bitterly, her gaze once again dropping to her lap, "Horace lived nearby. He was a neighbor. When our parents died, an officer was threatening to put Sarah in an orphanage—said I wasn't old enough to take care of her by myself, and I wasn't married. Horace offered to marry me so they wouldn't take Sarah away." She scoffed, "It wasn't until later, after I had... well, I found out that that probably wouldn't have happened. Horace wanted my parent's money and was working with the officer to pressure me."

Nate didn't answer immediately; he had thought that someone who would beat a little girl was bad enough, but this... he wasn't so naïve to believe that evil didn't happen in the world—he had, after all, just robbed a bank a few days beforehand—but, there was a part of him that didn't want to admit that things like that could happen. Especially with a lawman involved like that. He finally blew out a long breath, and answered honestly, "Not gonna lie to you, Ma'am... If'n he was still alive, I'd probably go shoot him myself."

Mary looked up once more, a hint of a smile on her tear streaked face, "Thanks, Nate." She wiped at the tears, "I probably better get some sleep now."

She laid down, snuggling up close to her sister while Nate carefully put the fire out and wrapped himself in his coat. As he lay there staring at the stars, the owl continued to question him from the darkness. *Hoo... Hoo.*

Who was he? Who was she? He considered the owl's question for a long time before he finally found sleep.

***** ******

FIVE

Nate woke to the distant sound of birds chirping and lay quietly, shivering in the cold as he stared up at the sky. He could tell it was lighter to the east and figured it was getting close to dawn. He stretched lightly, once again wishing he'd thought to grab an extra blanket; his muscles were stiff and sore from the cold air. He knew the only way he was going to warm up was by moving, so he pulled himself painfully into a sitting position and looked across the remains of the fire. Mary and Clara's forms were cuddled together on the other side of it, under the blanket—probably a lot warmer than he was at the moment.

He watched them for a few moments, thinking about their conversation. He didn't know what to make of her story—much less what he should do in light of it. After everything she had told him last night... he wasn't going to lie, he had a few concerns... but it wasn't like he had room to judge. She at least had a legitimate reason for what she'd done—he'd just been stupid.

The soft trickle of water from the creek wasn't enough to mask the occasional deep rumble of thunder in the distance. He rolled his eyes; the last thing they needed was a rainstorm. He shook out his boots, and paused for a moment, stretching out his feet as he noticed a hole in the toe of his left sock. He wriggled his toes, staring at the hole before shrugging it off. It was better than a hole in his head. He grinned at the thought and shook his head, pulling his boot on. He'd have to sew the sock when he had time... and that wasn't today.

He stood and stretched, clapping his arms to get the blood circulating before lighting the twigs and bark he'd left near the fire. Once the small fire was going, he grabbed the pot and started for the creek.

By the time he got back, the small fire was blazing merrily—Mary was up, crouched near the fire feeding more sticks into it—and he set the pot of water next to it, hoping it would heat quickly. He grinned, "Morning, Ma'am... I figured a cup of hot tea would warm y'all up before moving out."

"Thank you." She answered softly, still looking at the fire. Once she finished feeding her pile of sticks into the fire, she stood and shuffled back to the blanket roll and woke Clara up. The little girl tried to cling to the blankets, but Mary pried her hands loose and half drug and half carried the sleepy girl toward the creek while he waited for the water to boil.

They ate the last of the turkey with a cup of tea before moving out. Nate half hoped they would make a small town, but there was a part of him now that wasn't in as much of a hurry as he had been.

And he didn't quite know what to think of that.

***** ******

Mary held tightly to Clara as Nate led the horse down a steep incline.

She felt sick—she shouldn't have told Nate everything last night. She hadn't said anything to anyone for all this time, and now she just blurted it all out like that. Who knew what he thought of her now— he'd barely said a word all day.

She frowned as she waved off a fly buzzing by her ear. Not that he had room to judge, but still.

Of course, it wasn't like he was being mean or rude. Just silent. Maybe he was just focused on the journey? It wasn't like he had been overly talkative yesterday either.

She shook her head in disgust. Maybe she should just stop worrying so much.

She snorted a quick laugh at that thought. Now she had to deal with the fact that someone knew her secret. Even if Nate didn't tell the law, he might accidentally say something that would start questions.

She huffed out a breath in frustration. Her problem was that she had too much time to think. Too much time to mull over everything and drive herself crazy. Just sitting in the back of the horse, clutching Clara to make sure she didn't fall off. If she had someone to talk to, it would pass time faster. Unfortunately, it had been a long time since she could really talk to anyone.

She glanced up at Nate. He was walking steady as he led the horse, but she knew that he had to be tired of walking by now. She had to admit it would be difficult for him to focus on the path he was leading if he was trying to hold a conversation with her, so his lack of talking was understandable.

As he led the horse along, she watched him and wondered what he thought about while he walked.

***** ******

They stopped for the night and made camp in a small grove of trees. Nate was looking forward to the chance to talk with Mary... he'd been mulling over their situation all day long and had a possible solution... but leading a horse didn't give him much of a chance to converse.

Well, that and he didn't want to say much in front of Clara. The little girl had been through a lot and he didn't want to bring it back up.

He watered the horse and made certain it had plenty of grass before lighting a small fire. Mary and Clara had taken the pan and were picking blackberries from a large thicket. By the time the fire was burning, they had the pan almost full, so they all sat around eating berries until darkness fell.

Mary had bundled up her daughter—sister, he corrected himself—in the blankets, and the girl was asleep almost immediately.

Unfortunately, it was about that time that he lost his nerve. He grabbed a piece of wood and started whittling. He was trying to make a doll for Clara. He figured if he could make a head and body, she might use a piece of old cloth for a dress or something. If he could just get it to look right.

And not like a pinecone.

He chuckled softly to himself and continued whittling. He was trying to build up the nerve to say something, but he was still worried. How would she respond?

In the end it was up to her. He could always light a shuck for Mexico in the hopes they wouldn't catch him. She had to worry about her sister.

He cast a furtive glance in her direction and tightened his jaw. How should he broach the subject?

***** ******

Mary watched as the orange flames of the small fire danced against the dark background of rocks. She would have felt safer with a large fire, like the ones they'd had on the wagon train the first few weeks. The call of wolves and coyotes throughout the night always scared her, especially since Nate insisted on putting out the fire before they went to sleep—she worried that something would creep into the camp and drag Clara off in the middle of the night.

"So, ya'll were heading for California?"

She looked up from the fire; Nate had been whittling a chunk of wood with a small knife, but had paused, watching her questioningly. "Uh, yes." She shrugged noncommittally, "It just seemed like the furthest place from home we could go would be the safest."

"Yeah." Nate nodded slowly and went back to whittling. "I reckon that makes sense."

Mary watched him for a few moments as he worked at the... well, if she were honest, she'd have to admit that she had no idea what he was working at. It was about the size of his hand, and he'd been working at it all evening. She finally asked, "How about you?"

He paused again, meeting her gaze, "To be honest, I don't rightly know. I came west to be a man..." He reddened slightly—even in the dim light she could tell. "When my Pa finally got home after the war, he told me I was worthless and needed to make something of myself. So, I left home and came west." He shrugged, "I've been moving west for the past six years with nothing to show for it but a lynch mob on my trail."

Mary tilted her head, confused. He didn't look that old. "You've been moving west for six years? How old are you?"

He grinned, "Twenty on my last birthday, but that was a while back."

"You left home to be a man at fourteen?"

Nate chuckled, "Yes, Ma'am... I reckon Pa had high expectations."

"Fourteen was pretty high of an expectation."

"I dunno, I knew a few boys my age that went off to fight. With Pa gone, I thought I oughta stay with my Ma—she was sickly—but she died a month before Pa got back." He shrugged and went back to whittling, "I guess that's what bothered him the most, her dying whilst he was gone."

"I suppose that would be hard." She tossed a small stick in the fire, sending up a shower of sparks. "Our parents died together." At his questioning glance, she added; "They had gone out for a drive in the country and the horses broke loose from the buggy. It hit a tree and killed them both."

"Sorry to hear that." Nate looked down at his lap, "Rough for you both." He whittled on the wood for a moment, "And that's when... *he* came 'round?"

"Yeah..." She offered simply and looked down at her lap. There wasn't really anything else to say about it... she'd told him how it ended last night.

She heard Nate stand and move closer to the fire, but she didn't look up. He poured some tea into his cup and sat across from her, throwing a few twigs into the fire. He was silent for a full minute before he blurted, "Ma'am... Mary? What are we going to tell people?"

Mary looked up from her lap and lifted an eyebrow slowly, "What do you mean?"

"Well..." He paused, rolling a twig between his fingers, "You're wanting to hide who you are, and I'm wanting to hide who I am... that just might be difficult."

Mary sat back, curious, "Why do you say that?"

Nate blew out a breath and dropped the twig into the fire. "If the law comes looking for you, they might track you to the wagon train. If the posse that was after me made it to the wagon train... well, that would make it the last place they knew I was."

He trailed off for a moment, watching her. She nodded simply, not really seeing where he was going with it. "Ok..."

"Well, if we pop up somewhere and tell them we were survivors of that wagon train, that might attract attention. Someone may put two and two together."

"Oh!" Mary exclaimed, finally seeing where he was going with it. "I..." She grimaced in frustration. She had been thinking about it herself but hadn't come up with a solution yet. It was inexcusable, but with constantly worrying about the Indian's attacking again, and then traveling so long... and now worrying about how much she had shared with Nate...

And she should have, for Clara's sake, if for no other reason. "What do you think we should do?"

Nate shrugged, "Well, I reckon that the best way to hide who you are is for people to think you're someone else that's come from someplace else."

Mary nodded slowly, "Yes... That's true." When her and Clara had traveled west, she had worked to make certain that people believed them to be from Virginia. She had even practiced an accent that was more indicative of coming from there... one that, now that she thought of it, she had forgotten to maintain with all of the stress and fear of the past several days.

"Well, that's what I wanted to talk to you about. I was thinking..." He looked down at the fire, "I mean, some are gonna be looking for a man by himself, and others might be looking for a woman with a little girl, but..." He trailed off, obviously embarrassed.

She could feel her face heat up, "But, nobody's going to be looking for a family." She finished for him.

Nate looked up and stared at her for several seconds before nodding slowly, "Yes, Ma'am. They wouldn't suspect that a family traveling together—a husband and wife with a child—are the people they are looking for."

Her face still hot, she set her jaw. "You want to get married?"

"No!" He almost shouted, gesturing wildly with his hand as he hurriedly explained, "No, I meant we could pretend to be husband and wife as we travel. Just something to tell people so's they wouldn't think... I wasn't expecting you to..." He looked down at his lap—if it were possible, even more embarrassed than before.

"Oh." She felt her face burn again. Her only experience with a man asking for her to marry him for convenience hadn't turned out too well, but Nate seemed so earnest. "I'm sorry, I didn't mean to..."

"That's ok, Ma'am..." He cut her off, "You don't know me, and you've had some bad experiences—but I figured I can get you where you're going, and that'll keep both of us safe."

Mary nodded slowly, "Ok." She gestured absently between them. "I agree. It's mutually beneficial." She thought for a moment, "But we need to make it believable. We'll need to have our story straight before we talk to anyone."

Nate nodded, "Well, I s'pose the first thing we need to do is agree on a name... a surname anyway. I'm using my middle name for now, and you two... well, no sense in everyone changing up first names again."

Mary tilted her head to the side, "Nate's your middle name? What's your first name?"

"Japheth." He shrugged absently, "Ma named me after one of Noah's sons."

"Biblical name... that's nice." She waved dismissively, "But I agree, keep the names we're using, and choose a new surname. But there are two problems. First, it'll have to be something you can remember to spout off in a hurry. Then it'll also have to be something believable. We couldn't use a name that makes us sound like one of those Chinese launderers."

Nate tilted his head thoughtfully, "Few years ago, I worked at a ranch that had a Chinese cook. Nice fella. I was gonna suggest we use his name, but that would be Wong."

It took her several moments before she realized he was making a joke. She picked up a small stick and threw it across the fire at him, "That was horrible."

Nate grinned, "I thought it was funny."

Mary rolled her eyes, "Alright, Mr. Wong, where are we from?"

Nate thought for a moment, "Wherever you want."

"Well, no—it has to be somewhere you've at least visited." At his questioning glance she added, "Imagine telling someone you were from Georgia, and trying to think of an answer when they ask where at there? It can get scary when someone came from the same town you say you're from and tries to pinpoint if you were their neighbor." She knew that from experience.

Nate shook his head slowly, "I see what you mean, but it just doesn't always happen like that." He shrugged and picked up another twig, nervously twirling it in his fingers, "I've never been asked where I was from."

"Well, I wouldn't count on that if we are posing as a married couple. That's a tad different than an..." She trailed off, suddenly feeling awkward.

"You can say it. Outlaw."

"I was going to say single man." She offered defensively.

"Right." He cleared his throat, "Anyway, I was thinking about what you said with the surname, and to be honest, I don't think mine is known." He chewed on his bottom lip for a moment, "I mean, I don't think that even Hank, Simmons, or Jed knew my surname. It may be just as easy to use Taylor."

"Alright, the Taylor family from... where? Virginia?"

"How about Pennsylvania?"

Mary felt a quick chill run through her, "No, not Pennsylvania... What's wrong with Virginia?"

Nate shrugged, "I'm from there. Well, kind of—small town on the border of Maryland."

"We can be from the southern part of it."

He shrugged, "Ok, what did I do? Farmer?"

"That would fit. Family farm, we headed west, and..." She tilted her head to the side, "Not Indians... that's too close to the truth."

"Wagon swept downstream at a crossing." Nate shook his head sadly, "Seen it happen. No time to get anything out, and we barely got our... daughter out."

"That about covers it."

"Now we'll need an outfit. Can't share one horse to California."

"Now how do you propose to do that?" She grimaced at the pun, but plowed ahead, "I left almost everything back at the wagon." She held up her small bag, "I have a few odds and ends, and about sixteen dollars, left." She thought for a moment, "I have my Pa's watch that I *could* sell, if we need..."

"No," He hurriedly cut her off, "I'll come up with something. The last thing you need to do is sell the only heirloom you have from your father."

She felt a rush of appreciation—it was thoughtful of him to consider something like that, given the circumstances.

Nate had continued, "I have three dollars myself... and a few bits. We might be able to get to California with that."

"Too bad you left that bag of gold back there, eh?" She offered sardonically.

Nate lifted an eyebrow, but grinned when he noticed her smile. "Ha ha."

Mary shook her head, "Well, jokes aside..." She pointed to the set of saddlebags that Clara was using for a pillow, "Have you gone through those?"

Nate reddened slightly, "Well, no Ma'am... not really. I looked to see if there was anything we could use—I was hoping for more shells for the rifle—but it was just personal papers and whatnot..." He paused for a moment, then added, "Well, there was also a Bible— but as far as the papers, I didn't want to pry into someone's business."

"Well, I understand... but those papers belong to someone who has passed—there could be something of use."

"True, I s'pose." Nate sighed, "I guess we could look."

Mary stood and moved over to where Clara lay sleeping. "Hang on." Nate spoke softly as he moved around the fire. He pulled off his coat and offered it to her.

Nodding gratefully, she folded it neatly and lifted Clara's head, exchanging the coat for the saddlebags.

She handed the saddlebags to Nate, who moved back to the fire and started pulling out odds and ends. The Bible he sat gently on a rock. After that there were several letters, a book of poetry, a few handkerchiefs, and a small purse that jingled softly when he moved it.

"Well, that's a good sign..." She offered hopefully. Not that she felt good about using someone else's money, but the person who owned it was dead, and they were not.

Nate opened the purse and shook the contents onto the ground. Three heavy gold coins fell out with a soft thud, followed by several two-bit coins. Frowning, he reached in and pulled out a wad of paper money. "Greenbacks..." He muttered, looking into the purse. "That's all of it." He fanned through it quickly. "Three hundred dollars cash." Nate looked up, "Plus the eagles—almost four hundred total. That's a lot of cash money."

Mary pursed her lips, "Not so much. I spent almost that much on the trip west for the two of us... and I didn't even have to buy a wagon. It'd be most of a thousand dollars to buy everything we'd need."

Nate nodded absently, "True."

"Well, if you can get us safely to a small town, we can try to get with another wagon train headed west."

Nate tilted his head, "Out of curiosity, why hadn't you thought of a railcar?"

"I thought of it." She looked down at Clara, who was sleeping peacefully, "It would've been faster... and maybe even cheaper... but I didn't have enough money at first. It was over a hundred dollars a ticket..." She shrugged absently, "Well, also I thought it'd be the first place the Pink's would look for me." She blew out a long breath, "As I worked and saved up, the people I worked around were all talking about the wagon trains... how it was so adventurous... I found out I could pay a little to travel with someone and still have money left over to start with. The Rothards—the family I was traveling with—She was pregnant with her third child. I was helping as a nanny."

Nate nodded, "Yeah, I can see that. But now..." He picked up the coins, shoving them and the greenbacks back into the purse. "Now a ticket would be a safer bet. There's the cash for it." He offered her the purse.

She took the purse carefully, "You want me to hold it?"

Nate chuckled softly, "Well, Ma'am... I figgered you needed it more than me. If something happens and the posse... well, if something happens, I can get by."

She nodded slowly, "Thanks, Nate."

They stood awkwardly staring at each other for a moment when the fire popped, sending showers of sparks into the air, and causing her to jump slightly as a hot cinder landed on her sleeve.

Nate reached over quickly and brushed it off her sleeve—then blushed and stepped back, "Sorry 'bout that, Ma'am. Didn't want you burnt." He blew out a quick breath, "I reckon it's time to get some rest. Long day tomorrow." He moved back over to the other side of the fire and sat down.

Taking his cue, she laid down next to Clara, using an edge of the blanket to cover herself. "Goodnight, Nate."

"'night Ma'am."

She watched as he started to cover the fire with dirt, "Nate?" She barely choked his name out, "Could you leave it... for just a little while longer? Until I'm asleep?"

"Yes'm."

She curled closer to Clara and listened to the crackling sound of the fire. After a few minutes it was joined by the scraping of wood as Nate continued whittling.

She lay listening for a long time before falling asleep.

***** ******

SIX

Mary woke up late that next morning and immediately panicked when she noticed Clara wasn't in her bedroll. She sat up, looking frantically for her—relaxing with relief when she spotted her sitting across the fire, holding what looked like a doll.

She rubbed her eyes and looked around, confused. She didn't see Nate anywhere. She looked back at Clara, "Where's Nate?"

The little girl grinned widely and pointed toward the woods where a small creek ran through.

"Is Nate cleaning up?"

Clara nodded, then jumped up and came around the fire, plopping down on the blanket next to her. She was clutching a doll in her hands like she thought it would disappear.

"Hey, Clara... what's that?" Mary smiled as Clara held the doll out for her. She took it gently, looking it over. "Did Nate give you this?"

Clara's smile widened even further, and she nodded vigorously.

Mary grinned at the girl's exuberance and studied the doll. Now she knew what he'd been whittling all that time. He had carved it from wood and used a couple handkerchiefs to make a dress, as well as a makeshift scarf for its head. She felt a burning at the corner of her eyes as tears threatened to start. He had obviously put a lot of effort into it. He had tried for some detail on the dolls face to make it more doll-like; even hollowing out little dimples on the face and burning the center of them so they looked more like eyes. If she were honest, it wasn't the most beautiful doll in the world—he really wasn't that good at whittling—but, she could tell by Clara's expression that *she* thought it was the best doll she'd ever had.

And that was all that mattered.

"That was very sweet of him." She passed the doll back to Clara with a smile. "He seems very nice, doesn't he?"

Clara nodded enthusiastically and clutched the doll to her chest. Her face tightened suddenly, and she exploded with a tiny sneeze *"Choo!"*

Mary immediately handed her a handkerchief, "Here, sweetie, wipe your nose." She felt the girls head,

"Well, still no fever—but we'll need to get you indoors soon."

Clara nodded and then scampered off to play with her doll.

Mary watched her run off, hoping again that it was just a chill and not something more insidious. Little kids were resilient, and she hoped Clara was no exception. She just hoped they found a town soon.

She blew out a long breath and turned to face the fire, noticing that Nate had already put water on to boil. Not knowing how long he would be gone she started to make some tea—which was the one thing they had plenty of—and waited for him to get back.

By the time Nate got back, she was drinking a strong cup of tea and eating blackberries.

"Morning, Ma'am." Nate grinned as he filled his cup, "Y'all 'bout ready to go?"

She popped another berry in her mouth and smiled. "I'd love a couple eggs first... and maybe some ham." She thought for a moment, "And maybe a pillow to sit on."

Nate blushed a bright red, "Well, I can't help the seating arrangements, but I'll see what I can spot for dinner tonight if we don't find a town." He looked up at the sky, "We've been traveling nigh onto three days— probably covered seventy miles at least. We should be coming close to something." He took a sip of the tea, "Either way, we'll stop early enough to get some food."

Mary nodded, "Thanks. I was hoping we'd find a town soon—I think Clara may be coming down with something from all the night air."

He looked over at Clara who was trying to feed her new doll a berry. "Yes'm. Soon as y'all are ready, we can get going."

Mary stood, not looking forward to another day in the saddle, "Alright, we'll just be a few minutes then." She motioned to Clara and headed down toward the creek.

***** ******

They packed up the camp and rode out while the morning breeze was still cool on their faces.

The hours blended into each other as they slowly moved northeast. They hadn't spotted a single person since the wagon train, but she thought that was for the best. She knew Nate was hoping that the posse would give up looking for him, especially since he left the gold back at the wagon train—but, if people started talking about seeing someone of the same description out on the prairie...

She shook off that thought and watched the slowly passing scenery. It had been like this on the wagon train—day after day without seeing anything but grass and trees. It was rough country out here.

Unfortunately, with little to keep her occupied, she found herself fretting constantly about what might happen next. Part of it was concern about heading east—which was bad enough—but on top of that they planned to catch a train. She had avoided trains before because she was worried about the Pinks, and had a hard time believing it was safer now than a few weeks ago... but the fact was, she had been on the run for months and they hadn't found her yet. And even if they had been tracking her, the trail would end with the wagon train and not at a train depot a hundred miles away.

And definitely not for a woman with her husband. That was another plus.

The horse stumbled, jerking her sharply to the side. "Ouch!" Mary cried out as the sudden shift jammed the saddle horn into her leg.

"You alright, Ma'am?" Nate had stopped the horse and was looking back at her with a concerned look on his face.

"Just jammed my leg is all. We're fine." Clara was actually asleep, and even her cry hadn't woken her.

"Alright, just hang on." He gestured to the trail ahead that had taken a decidedly downhill turn, "It may get rough for a few."

Mary nodded and set her jaw as they moved out again. Her leg smarted, and she didn't like the memories it dredged up—it was the same spot Horace had hit her one time while they were riding in the buggy back home.

They had been out for a ride to see a friend of his, and he'd gotten mad at something—for the life of her, she couldn't remember what—and he'd hit her in the back, knocking her to the ground. She had cried almost all the way home, but as they neared some neighbors, he suddenly got self-conscious and wanted her to smile. When she didn't smile immediately, he'd hit her in the leg... hard. It had hurt for weeks, even after she'd...

Well, left him.

It was strange to think about being married to him to begin with. Of course, now she knew all he was after was money, but she was thankful that had been as far as his interest went. He'd taken no interest in her beyond having her keep house and watch Sarah... Clara, she corrected herself. He hadn't even shared a room with her. She hadn't realized how abnormal that was until well after she was gone. If people had known that she and Horace hadn't slept in the same room, they'd have known their marriage had been a farce...

A cold chill swept through her at that sudden revelation. Here she was with another farcical marriage—one that her life counted on to portray as real. That meant wherever she and Nate went, as long as they were pretending to be married, they would have to stay in the same room.

She looked ahead at Nate—a bank robber, maybe—but he was a good guy. How was he going to react to that?

***** ******

Nate grimaced as another sharp rock poked into his foot. The rate he was going, he was going to need new boots before long. He looked down at his clothes—torn jeans, worn boots—at least the shirt looked alright, but he looked a mess. He needed a bath and a new outfit, not just the boots. He wondered what people would think of him when they strolled into town.

Of course, it didn't really matter what his clothes looked like. All most of 'em would pay attention to was that he was married to a pretty girl, and he could think of worse things for people to think about him than that.

His smile faded as he thought of Hank, Simmons, and Jed. They would never know what it was like to even pretend to be married to a pretty girl, much less anything else. They were all pushing daisies from the underside while he calmly walked away from it all.

'Course, he knew that wasn't exactly the way of it. They were on that path long before he'd started running with them. Come to think of it, he'd probably kept them out of trouble.

But they were still dead, and he wasn't.

He shook off that line of thought. It wasn't helping him to think like that—it wasn't going to bring them back. He just needed to push forward and be different.

When he was a boy, back before his Ma died, there'd been a steady stream of neighbors that'd come around to get advice from her. She always had the same answer every time someone got sideways in their life. Always quiet and demure, she would pour them tea and quietly ask, *"What about Jesus? Have you asked him what to do?"*

He supposed that's what he ought to do—talk to Jesus—but felt ashamed to do it. Like he was just asking 'cause he was in trouble. He never wanted to be that type.

The question was, what type did he want to be?

***** ******

Mary watched Nate as he led the horse slowly down a short slope. She was waiting—somewhat impatiently—for an opportunity to talk to him about their cover story. Clara had fallen asleep—as only a child can in such an uncomfortable position—so she thought now would be the best time.

But he didn't look like he was stopping anytime soon.

What made it worse was the knowledge that every step they took brought them closer to a town, and she needed to set this straight now. She'd been fretting so long her stomach was aching.

She waited a few more minutes before finally deciding to just stop him. "Nate?" Mary barely choked the word out, but as soon as she said it, she wanted to take it back. How would he react? What would he say? What would he do? Would he turn into Horace?

Nate didn't turn to face her, as he was focusing on picking his way down the rocky slope, but called over his shoulder, "Ma'am?"

She swallowed hard and decided to just push ahead. "I... we need to talk."

He looked back over his shoulder, his eyebrow lifted, "Yes, Ma'am..." He nodded curtly and stopped the horse, patting its muzzle to hold it still, "You need a break?"

"No," She spoke from the saddle, not wanting to take the time to get down. "Well, maybe... but we need to talk... before we get to a town."

He lifted his eyebrow again and nodded slowly, "Alright."

"I..." She bit her lip, "I'm worried about getting caught."

"Well, Ma'am," Nate chuckled softly, waving off a fly that was buzzing near his face, "I reckon I know how you feel there, but I think we'll be fine if'n we stick together."

She felt her face flush hot, "That's what I wanted to talk to you about. I was thinking..." She looked down at the rocks below, "I mean, you said it yourself that nobody's going to be looking for a family." She set her jaw and looked up, meeting his eyes. "But if that family isn't acting like one..."

Nate stared at her for several seconds before lifting an eyebrow once more. "Ma'am?"

She looked down again, unable to meet his gaze as she explained, "They wouldn't suspect that a husband and wife are the people they are looking for... unless they aren't acting like a husband and wife." She looked up defiantly, "We'll need to stay in the same room."

His face turned beet red and both eyebrows flew up, "Ma'am?"

"You'd be on the floor." She hurriedly explained, "We just can't pretend to be husband and wife as we travel and stay in separate rooms. Nobody would believe it."

"Oh." He flushed an even deeper shade of red, "Sorry. I didn't..."

She waved dismissively, trying to look indifferent to the situation, hoping a casual demeanor would calm him down. "I understand, but I think it will be safest."

Nate nodded slowly, but he looked unconvinced. "Yes'm... I s'pose." He looked around, "Did you still need a break?"

She glanced down at Clara, who hadn't stirred, "No, let's push on for now." She wouldn't have minded stretching her legs, but she knew that he would probably want to talk about the situation... Pushing on would give her more time to think about it.

"Alright." He turned and started leading the horse again.

Frowning, Mary watched him as he continued down the trail. Things had just started to look like they would work out, and she hoped this didn't cause problems.

***** ******

SEVEN

Nate stared out over the wide plains; his eyes drawn to a pair of small birds as they arced across the sky chasing insects. Like everything else out here, they were oblivious to his presence as he watched. The bird's shrill whistles reminded him of happy children playing.

Of happier times. Like when he wasn't running from a noose, happier.

He dropped the reins to let Rico—what he had taken to calling the horse—continue grazing hungrily on the lush grass. He closed his eyes and breathed in deeply, focused on the fragrance and sounds as he waited for Mary. She had taken Clara down to a small stream near a clump of nearby trees. They had spotted a town up ahead and wanted to look somewhat presentable before arriving.

Sighing in contentment, he opened his eyes and scanned the horizon. The small town was maybe five or six miles away... he had a hard time gauging distances on the plain like this. It wouldn't take them long to get there though. They would definitely make it before the sun dropped behind the horizon.

Looking past the town, seemingly hundreds of miles away—it was almost like looking at the other side of the world—great grey clouds billowed toward the heavens. He sighed deeply, appreciating the view... really, this was one of the most beautiful places he'd ever been.

"I could live here." Mary's quiet voice sounded right behind him.

Nate smiled, turning to face her. She stood a few feet away, her eyes focused on the horizon. He gestured toward Clara, who was chasing a butterfly through the grass. "We'll be in town soon. Maybe two hours or so. Is she ready for that?"

"I'm ready." She grinned, "Honestly, I think she believes this is one big adventure, but she'll be fine."

"Yeah, I see that." He watched the little girl as she tripped, rolling in the grass and jumping back to her feet to continue the chase. "Kids are resilient." He blew out a long breath and gestured at the slowly retreating horse. "We best get moving; I want to make it to town early enough to settle in. The later we are, the more likely we are to draw unwanted attention."

Mary nodded slowly, her jaw taut, "If our story is believable enough, we shouldn't."

Nate looked curiously at her, "You doubt the story?"

She grunted as a look of frustration crossed her face, "Yes... No... I don't know. I just want Clara safe."

Nate reached over and touched her arm reassuringly, "She will be. I will do whatever it takes to make certain of that."

Mary blinked her eyes slowly and whispered, "Alright. I believe you." She gave him a smile that he felt was forced, then nodded toward the horse that was almost fifty feet away and still moving. "I'll get Clara, but you best get the horse before it gets away."

Chuckling, Nate started after the horse, hoping nothing spooked it suddenly before he caught up to it. He had meant what he said. He was willing to do whatever it took to keep them safe... he just hoped that he could avoid a noose long enough to keep that promise.

***** ******

Mary looked around curiously as they rode through the sleepy looking town. She could see a few dogs in the street, and a large man standing by a barn at the far end, but there wasn't anyone else in sight.

Nate stopped the horse in front of a wide building with a large sign identifying it as the store. He tied the horse to the rail and turned back to face her. "Ok, you know the story, right?"

Struggling to keep from rolling her eyes, she smiled, "Yes, Nate... remember, I'm the one who came up with the story."

"I just wanted to check." He held out his arms, and she passed Clara down before allowing Nate to help her to the ground.

They hadn't made it seven steps into the store before a large woman burst from the back room, startling them.

"Helloooooo..."

Mary recoiled slightly; the woman's voice was more of a high-pitched trilling that hurt her ears.

"Um, hello." Nate smiled awkwardly as the woman neared.

"How *can* I help you... oh, bless my *SOUL*, lookit here!" She stopped, staring down at Clara, who was gaping openly at the woman with undisguised astonishment. "She is *so* cute!" The woman moved close, almost knocking Mary over as she knelt down to Clara's level, "What is *your* name, child?"

Clara grinned, obviously liking the woman, and looked up at Mary.

"Her name is Clara..." Mary offered quietly, "She doesn't talk."

"Oh, *my*! The *poor dear*!" She patted Clara on the shoulder, her meaty arm almost knocking the little girl to the ground, "Well, I'm Matilda... and I am *so* glad to meet you." She stood quickly, which thoroughly amazed Mary that she could move that much bulk so quickly. "I'll tell you what, little Clara... you just go over to that candy jar and get yourself a big licorice. My treat!"

Clara looked up to Mary with a questioning glance, and Mary tilted her head, "Are you sure?"

"ABSOLUTELY!" Matilda thundered, as she moved across the store, "Matter of fact, honey... take a few!" She grabbed the candy jar and reached in, grabbing out a small handful and shoving them in Clara's hand. "There you go!" She popped one of the candies into her mouth and sat the jar back on the counter before looking back at Nate, "So, how can I help you?"

Mary found herself smiling at the woman's overzealous friendliness.

Nate spoke softly, "Well, Ma'am... we need a few supplies." He paused for a moment before continuing, "We lost our wagon, and most of our supplies crossing a river a few days ago..."

"Oh my *SOUL!*" Matilda exclaimed, her hands both going to her mouth. "You poor dears! What happened?"

As she spoke, a thin man walked from the back room, wiping his hands on his apron, "What happened to what, dearest?"

"Amos! These poor people lost their wagon in the river, and this poor child is so upset that she won't even talk anymore!"

Mary suppressed a grin at the woman's exuberance as she took the story and drew her own conclusions.

Nate turned to face the thin man, "We're heading west—been seeing some beautiful country as we travelled so we broke off from the wagon train and started scoping out the land—we seriously thought about stopping and settling down, but in the end we decided to look a bit longer. Few days ago, we were crossing a river..." Nate trailed off and blew out a breath before he continued, "Well, the yoke broke, and the horses spooked—they went one way, and the wagon went another."

The thin man nodded knowingly, "We've seen it firsthand on the way here... happens more often than you'd think." He lowered his voice, and Mary could barely hear him, "Did you lose anyone?"

Nate shook his head, "Thankfully, no. Just the stuff."

"Praise the Lord for that." He looked out the front window and gave a half-shrug, "Well sir, I don't know anyone with a wagon for sale, plus it's getting late in the day—too late to go anywhere even if you did get an outfit. Next stage is tomorrow afternoon. You can get a room in the hotel for now, take a load off your mind and get cleaned up, then you can plan your next step from there."

Nate looked over at Mary and nodded, "Does that sound good... sweetheart?"

The endearment was so unexpected that Mary barely contained a gasp, but she recovered quickly, "We need a bath, so that would be wonderful!"

Matilda guffawed loudly, "Ha! Just like a woman! Forget the junk we didn't need and get me a bath!" She turned and walked back toward the counter, "You just come with me, and I'll get you and the little one fixed up with a change of clothes and some toiletries." She started humming loudly as she rummaged through a box, digging out items and setting them on the counter. "Ooh, and dearie I have got the *perfect* dress for you!" She clucked her tongue and shuffled quickly across the room, "I wanted to wear it, but there was no way it was going to fit me, and that's the truth!"

Mary watched in amazement as Matilda twirled her large girth up and down the aisles, gathering things she thought they needed while Nate watched helplessly.

By the time she finished, they all had fresh clothing and some basic supplies. Nate paid for them with a tight look, scooped the bundle from the counter, and herded them toward the door. "Alright, we'll get a room and be back tomorrow after we decide what we're doing."

"That will be great!" Matilda exclaimed as Nate opened the door. "You all get some rest!"

Nate waved acknowledgement as they exited the store and quickly crossed the street to the hotel. "That went well." He offered softly as they climbed up the steps to the boardwalk, "Now we'll just get a room, and we'll be able to plan better once we're clean and rested."

Mary clutched Clara's hand tightly as they entered the hotel. Within a few minutes they were on their way up the stairs to their room.

***** ******

Mary sat heavily on the bed, pulling uncomfortably at the collar of her new dress as she looked around the small room. She and Clara had both finished their baths and now they were waiting for Nate to return. Clara was standing by the window gazing out over the street, her tiny fists clutching the small wooden doll that Nate had made for her.

Mary was fairly certain that she was watching out for Nate.

She closed her eyes, wishing Horace had been more like Nate. It would've been nice to really be married to someone like him...

She shook her head, knowing full well that that wasn't going to happen. Nate seemed nice, but he was only helping her to save his own skin. As soon as they were clear of this area, he would be long gone.

No—she mentally berated herself—she wasn't being fair. There was more to Nate than that. There was something in him that wanted to do right... and the fact was he felt sorry for them... that's why he was helping, and that was the best she could expect from anyone.

She lay back on the bed, her eyes tracking a fly that was walking across the whitewashed ceiling. It would stop, then in a burst of energy walk several inches before stopping. She wondered absently what it hoped to accomplish on the ceiling—hopefully there wasn't any food up there for it to eat.

But, then again, it was better than it buzzing in her ear.

She shook her head, wondering what Nate was doing. He'd left for the bath house over an hour ago—more than long enough for him to get cleaned up and come back.

Unless he'd already taken off and left them... or was at the saloon.

That thought put a shock of fear through her so sharp that a part of her was hoping he had just ridden out.

But there was another part hoping he hadn't.

She tightened her jaw and squeezed her eyes shut to hold back tears that threatened to form. She needed to stop thinking like that. Whatever Nate did, he did, and that was all there was to it.

Plus, he had left all the money with her... so she wouldn't be too bad off, considering. She at least had a stake.

"Ugggh!" She hit the bed with both fists, frustrated with herself for her constant vacillation, and once again wondered how long Nate was going to be gone. She lay there for several seconds before feeling a sharp tug at her dress. Sitting up, she found Clara staring at her questioningly.

"Are you alright?"

Clara sniffed and rubbed her arm under her nose.

"Oh, sweetie, come here." She pulled Clara close and pressed the back of her hand to her forehead, "You're a tad warm. I don't know..." She patted the bed, "Come up here and lay down for a bit." It wasn't just that she was concerned with her sister's health; she was trying to be prepared if Nate *had* gone to the saloon and came back with... ideas.

Clara clambered up into the bed and curled into a tiny ball, hands still clenched around the little doll. She lay quietly for several seconds before her breathing evened out and her eyes drooped shut.

Within minutes the girl was sleeping soundly.

Mary shook her head at her sister's ability to fall asleep so quickly. She stood, careful to not wake the sleeping girl as she moved over to the chair by the window. Shaking her head, she dug in her small bag and pulled out her Pa's watch. She had been so busy the last few days she had forgotten to wind it. It was stuck on a quarter past three.

She glanced out the window, wondering what time it actually was...

Which led her to wonder when Nate was coming back.

***** ******

EIGHT

Nate leaned against the corral post and watched the horse as it drank greedily from the trough. He felt clean... cleaner than he had for a while anyway. The bath had felt heaven-sent—he had stayed extra-long in the hot water just to soak his feet, only leaving when the water started to cool. Not wanting to return directly to the hotel while Mary and Clara were getting cleaned up, he had wandered over to the corral to check on the horse.

It was a feeble excuse, but he'd needed some time to think. He was in a quandary and simply had no idea what he should do.

When he and Mary had planned their story, he had been certain they had thought out all the details. They had decided to stick with his surname, Taylor—he was fairly certain it wasn't known—but then fabricated a new family history for both of them. They had even come up with a detailed cover story about losing their wagon when it got swept downstream.

He'd gotten all the specifics down pat—but what he hadn't considered was where he was going to sleep, and that was a problem. The reality was that they weren't married, and even though they were pretending to be, he wasn't going to share a room with a lady he wasn't really married to.

He smiled grimly because it seemed almost funny. He'd robbed a bank and she'd killed her husband, and to top it all off, they were lying to everyone they met. Despite all of that, he could not, in good conscience, sleep in the same room with her.

It was an interesting contradiction of principles that he would reflect on at some later point, but it didn't change the fact that he wasn't going to do it. That was set in stone in his mind.

Unfortunately, small town people had nothing better to do than talk and gossip, and they always watched strangers like hawks. If they noticed that he wasn't sleeping in the same room, that would be noticeable, and that would start rumors—and that was something he didn't want either.

He grimaced in frustration, wondering what he should do.

"How's it goin'?"

Nate jumped involuntarily at the voice and turned. The stable boy was standing a few feet away, a weed firmly clenched between his teeth. "Well, goin' fine, I s'pose. How 'bout you?"

The boy spat the weed from his mouth and grinned, a gesture that lit his whole face. "I'm good." He pointed to the small brown horse, "That's a good horse. What's his name?"

"He sure is," Nate grinned widely. "We call him Rico."

"Rico... good name for a horse."

They lapsed into a comfortable silence as they watched the horse. Nate really didn't want to talk, so he kept his eyes on Rico, and after a time the boy got bored and wandered off.

Finally alone again, Nate looked slowly around the town, wondering why it was so quiet. Even podunk little Klein had a lot going on. It was almost like everyone was at Church, and it wasn't even Sunday...

His eyes narrowed as he suddenly realized what he needed to do.

***** ******

Nate sat in the chair across from the elderly Parson, holding his hat tightly with both hands. "Thank you for seeing me, Parson Hammond... I'll tell you, with everything that's happened in the last few days we've been constantly praising God that he saw fit to keep us safe... But we have had something that has concerned us for the last few weeks—something that I thought you might be able to help with."

Parson Hammond tilted his head slightly to the side, "A concern? Like a Biblical question?"

"Well, not exactly, sir." Nate looked down, partly out of shame for lying to the Parson... "We had stopped in Julesburg and received news from home. The Pastor who married us..." He shook his head sadly, "Well, he ran off with a woman from Church and became a drunkard."

Nate had thought this sounded egregious enough to spark some righteous indignation from the elderly Parson, but he wasn't prepared for the response he got.

"Oh my."

Nate looked up; Parson Hammond was leaning back in his chair, tears at the corner of both eyes. Alarmed, he sat forward, "Are you alright, Parson?"

Parson Hammond waved a hand dismissively, "Oh, yes. It just hurts when the Devil conquers a man of God and drags him into sin."

Nate looked back down sheepishly, "Well, yes. That was bad," He offered weakly, ashamed that he'd made Parson Hammond upset. He thought that he would be like the Preacher back home—full of self-righteous judgement—that way it'd be easy to tell the story of how bad the Preacher that married them was, allude to how spiritual he thought Parson Hammond was, and easily convince him to marry them.

But now, the man was emotionally crushed over the infidelity of a fictitious Preacher.

Parson Hammond dabbed at his eyes with his handkerchief, "I'm fine... anyway, what is your concern?"

Nate swallowed with difficulty, "Well, sir... me and my wife, well, it bothered us. Makes us feel that since he went off like that, that our marriage wasn't real... like we ain't really married." Nate paused at the irony—that had been the closest thing to a true statement he'd made during the entire story.

Parson Hammond chuckled softly, "I'm certain that God doesn't look at it like that."

Nate shifted awkwardly in his chair, "Well, yeah... but it's been really weighing on our minds, especially with all of the problems..." Nate shrugged, "Well, we promised each other that the first Parson we met, we ask him to remarry us."

The Parson frowned, and looked down at his coffee cup, "Well, that's unusual..."

"Yes, sir, but it's how we feel."

The Parson nodded slowly, "Well if it will help, go ahead and bring your wife over to the Church."

***** ******

Mary sat in the chair, listening to the low sounds of Clara's snores as she stared at her Pa's pocket-watch, her eyes tracking the slow hands as they moved around the dial. A sharp cough filtered through the wall, once again reminding her how thin the walls were—much like the boarding home she and Clara had stayed in back in St. Louis. There'd been a man downstairs who spent all evening practicing Shakespeare lines, hoping to one day act on Broadway in New York. She was fairly certain that even now she could quote most of Marc Antony's lines from Julius Caesar.

That memory brought a real smile to her face; the first she could remember in days... but that smile faded quickly at the sound of boots coming up the stairs. She didn't know why it made her nervous... it was probably the man from the hotel coming up to tell her that Nate had ridden out already. She cut her eyes over to her bag on the small stand; the money was still there...she'd seen it when she took out her Pa's watch.

She told herself it was a surprise that Nate left without taking it.

The sound of boots had reached the hallway and stopped in front of the door, followed by a sharp knock. Mary stood, resigned to the inevitable, and pulled the door open, surprised to see Nate standing in the hallway, out of breath.

"I need you to come with me." He breathed out the words in a sharp whisper.

She took a quick step backwards, "Why?"

He leaned in slightly, whispering again, "I want to get married."

Mary's hands flew to her mouth, and she stepped back further from the door, her legs bumping the bed in her haste to retreat, "You want to do what?"

Nate stepped further into the room, gesturing frantically, "*Shhhh.* Not so loud." He looked back into the hallway, then shut the door carefully before turning back to her. "I spoke with the Parson here—he's actually a really nice person—and asked him to marry us... well, again." He looked down sheepishly, "I told him we'd gotten word that the Preacher who'd married us fell off into sin, and we'd feel better if'n we were married by a true man of God."

Several things ran through her mind as she stood, staring at him... the first of which was surprise, followed by confusion. She had literally just resigned herself to the fact that Nate had taken the horse and fled town. Just showing back up at the hotel was more than she expected.

But now he was back, wanting to get married for real? That didn't make sense, except... her eyes cut to her bag and she knew he was just back for the money. She nodded slowly and sat down on the bed, careful to not wake Clara. "You can take the money that is left from the saddlebags... you don't have to keep up appearances for my sake."

Nate blinked twice before answering, "What?"

"You don't owe me anything." She gestured to her bag on the small stand, "You want the money? Just take it and go."

Nate's eyes narrowed, "I don't want to run off with the money... I want to get married."

Mary closed her eyes for a moment as a wave of emotion ran through her. She could not imagine what Nate was thinking—if it wasn't the money... what would an actual marriage get him? She opened her eyes, fixing them on his expectant face, "Why?"

Nate tightened his lips, standing silent for a moment before rubbing his eye with the back of his thumb. "Well, because we ain't really married...?" He shrugged weakly and looked down at the floor.

She snorted, "Well, I knew that, but why is it suddenly a problem? We've been pretending to be married all day."

Nate blew out a long breath, and leaned against the door, "I just don't feel that it's right."

"What's not right?"

"To stay in this room with you." He gestured to the room, "I don't feel right in here... with you... since we ain't married."

She looked around the small room, "Why not?"

"It ain't right."

She groaned, suddenly agitated. "Well, I'm not sure that shooting Horace was right either, but he's pushing up daisies regardless." She lifted an eyebrow, "And I don't honestly think that bank robbin' was high on the Lord's list of greatness either."

He looked back down at the floor, but not before she saw the hurt and disappointment on his face.

"Sorry." He mumbled softly. "I was just trying to... make it right."

Mary sat down, exasperated. She couldn't understand what his problem was. "Make what right, Nate? I don't get it. We're pretending to be married so you don't have to worry about getting hung. Don't you think that your feelings might pale in comparison?"

Nate drew in a breath, his lips a tight line as he watched her. After several seconds, he spoke softly, "Well, no Ma'am... I mean, we agreed to pretend to be married for safety—all our safety—not just mine... and meeting people out on the prairie was no problem. Here though..." He shook his head, and pointed at the floor, "I don't have any intentions beyond that spot on the floor, but here and any other town we'll be in, people will be watching. If they see us in separate rooms, that'll start talking. You said that yourself. All I'm wanting...all I'm asking is for you to marry me so we can stay in the same room without making my Ma roll over in her grave."

Mary stood there, her mind racing as she watched him. She could tell he was in earnest, and that spoke volumes for his character. She wanted to believe him, but she just didn't know. The last time she got married to someone she thought was being sweet... well, that didn't turn out too well.

She glanced back at Clara, curled up in the bed; her hand gripped tightly around the doll Nate had made her—and in a heartbeat made the decision. "Yes, I'll marry you."

Nate's head snapped up, his face hopeful, "You will?"

She nodded slowly as another wave emotion swept through her. "Yes." She couldn't have explained it to him, but it was that doll... that unasked and unnecessary gesture towards Clara that made up her mind.

And more importantly, made her willing to give him a chance.

***** ******

It took the Parson less than five minutes to pronounce them man and wife.

As Nate stood holding Mary's arm and listening to Parson Hammond quickly go through the vows, he realized the importance of what the Parson was asking.

...*Love, honor, protect, and cherish*... Deep down he realized that even though their marriage had initially been intended to make their continued travel arrangements moral, he couldn't leave it at that. He was making a solemn vow before God to keep her and Clara safe... and it was not a flippant agreement.

He had saved their lives at the wagon train and had been keeping her and her sister safe ever since. But this... he was reminded of a hero in a yellow-backed dime novel he'd read once. He had lived by some code of honor that said if you'd saved someone's life, you were responsible for them forever.

It hadn't made much sense to him at the time, mainly because it seemed like some deadbeat would use it as a way to sponge off the hero, but in this instance, right now, he could see a truth to it, a truth beyond the vain glory of a fictional hero. Despite all of his past choices, he desperately wanted to change. He wanted to be honorable.

So, when Parson Hammond asked if he would, he yelled, "I will!" so loudly that it caused Mary to jump and set the Parson's wife to giggling uncontrollably.

"Alright..." The Parson turned to Mary, "And will you, Mary Taylor, take Nathan Taylor to be your husband? To love, honor, and obey... in sickness and in health... as long as you both shall live?"

Mary glanced sideways at Nate, and then focused on the Parson, "I will."

The Parson smiled, "Then by the power vested in me by God in the sight of these witnesses, I now pronounce you man and wife." He glanced at Nate, "You may kiss your bride."

Nate felt his face heat up, but leaned over and gave Mary a quick peck on the cheek before thanking the Parson.

***** ******

Nate held the door open for Mary and Clara to enter, shutting the door carefully as he followed them in. They had eaten their celebratory meal at the restaurant, and with nothing else to do, retired to their room.

Mary sat heavily in the chair by the window. The sun was just dipping down below the horizon, casting a pallid orange glow to the room. She looked over at Nate and raised an eyebrow. "Well, we're married. Now what?"

"Well..." Nate leaned against the wall, "I think we probably ought to leave as soon as we can. The longer we stay, the more questions we'll draw."

Mary nodded slowly, "That's true." The last thing they needed were questions. "Then what?"

"We'll sell the horse and take the stage north into Wyoming. The rail line is not too long of a journey, and the trip to it will be comfortable enough by stage... at least in comparison to what we've been doing. With the money we have left, we should have no problem getting tickets to Sacramento."

Mary nodded slowly; her lips set in a straight line. She was worried on multiple levels, but even with those concerns, she was ready to go. She looked over at Clara, who had remained relatively unimpressed throughout the events of the day. She was still playing with the small wooden doll that Nate had carved her. "What do you think, Clara? Ready to go to California?"

The little girl shrugged absently without looking up. She still wasn't looking well—but she also had an attitude, which made it worse. Mary's mouth twisted into a half smile... Clara was still a tad grumpy after being woke up for the wedding.

"Well..." Nate gestured to the bedroll he had bought from the store, "We'll have to get up early in the morning. The holster said the stage comes through at sixish, and I'll need time to sell Rico before we go."

"Alright." She opened her mouth to say something else... thank him, maybe... something. But nothing came out.

She watched him spread out the bedroll in front of the door and lay down before she moved from the chair. "Come on, Clara. It's time to get some rest."

They both lay down on the bed, and Mary leaned over to blow out the lamp. As the final glow from the sun faded from the room, she found herself staring awkwardly at the ceiling. She didn't know what to do now that she had a husband, she didn't even know how she should feel about it. All she knew was that for the first time in a long time she did feel safer.

And that was all that mattered.

***** ******

The sun was barely peering over the horizon when they boarded the stage. Nate helped Mary through the door before handing Clara in to her. He paused before climbing in, staring at the slowly rising sun. They would reach the train within a few days, and then it was on to California. He had no idea what would happen once they got there, but this was at least a start. He nodded, more to himself than anything, and climbed into the stage.

***** ******

PART II

NINE

Nate struggled to keep from rolling his eyes as the dandy sitting across from them launched into yet another tale of how great he was. It had been the same thing, over and over again, since the man had boarded the stage thirty miles ago—well, the bragging coupled with the occasional flirting with Mary.

That part had flummoxed him; he'd been struggling with how to handle the situation. His first instinct was to punch the dandy in his smug little face, but starting trouble wasn't an option since he didn't want to draw attention to himself... but no man would let some dandy flirt with his wife, so that would draw attention as well.

He had tried taking the middle ground by reaching over and taking Mary's hand, holding it in—what he hoped was—an obvious show of affection... but that had almost backfired. Mary had jumped, obviously startled at first, but had settled back, evidently understanding his goal.

Unfortunately, that hadn't seemed to work, and the vile little dolt had continued his incessant bragging to get her attention.

"...of course, my wife and I won't settle out here. She was merely visiting family until I arrived. We will head back east..."

Nate bit his lip to hold back a sharp retort. He couldn't understand how the dandy could be openly forward with another woman, all the while talking about the woman he was supposed to be on his way to marry... Nate was trying to decide whether to lean across the narrow space and politely tell the man to shut up, or simply slap him across his flapping gums— feeling more disposed toward the latter—when Mary yawned widely, and turned to him, "Nate, darling... this trip has me so tired. I'm going to lay my head down for a while." She had taken to speaking with a southern drawl since they boarded the stage. That had thrown him off at first, but he was getting used to it.

But then Mary scooted closer to him and rested her head on his shoulder.

Nate involuntarily stiffened at the contact, but relaxed slowly, a smile tugging at the corner of his mouth at the crestfallen look on the dandy's face.

He looked at the seat next to him; Clara was pressed against the wall, her face impassive. "You doin' all right?"

Clara looked up and grinned sleepily, showing the gap between her teeth. She was still clutching the doll he had made for her. He'd offered to buy her a new one at the store, but she had refused the offer. He hadn't...

"Two minutes 'til Cobbinsville."

The loud call from the driver startled Mary, and she jumped, kicking the dandy hard in the shin.

He cursed loudly, rubbing his leg with a pained expression.

Mary leaned forward slightly, and with a thick southern drawl offered her apology. "Oh, sir... I am so sorry..." Her exaggerated reaction brought a smile to Nate's face, and he suspected that the kick hadn't been an accident.

After that the dandy fell quiet and started fidgeting. It was obvious that he was anxious... Nate was just glad that the man finally shut up for the first time in thirty miles.

The stage pulled into town with a loud yell from the driver, sliding to a sudden stop that jerked Nate's head forward. By the time he'd recovered, the stage door was jerked open, and the driver was yelling. "Alright people, welcome to Cobbinsville. You've got fifteen minutes or so while we change out the horses. That's enough time to get a bite at Maude's if'n you eat fast enough... and the outhouse is in the back..."

The driver was cut off as the young dandy burst from the stage, shoving him out of the way as he looked around wildly. "You said this is Cobbinsville, right?"

Nate slowly climbed out, watching the driver look the dandy up and down, wondering if the driver was going to slap the dandy for his impertinence, but the driver spoke softly, "Slow down there, sonny. What's your hurry?"

"Don't call me sonny." The dandy spoke haughtily as he gestured to the town, "I'm looking for Cobbins' Store."

The driver calmly gestured to the building not ten feet from them, "Sonny, it's right there. One of three whole businesses in town."

Without a word, the dandy turned and marched up the stairs and straight to the door.

The driver turned back, winking at Nate with a grin, "That one's a tad high strung, ain't he?"

Nate returned the grin, "Seems to be." He turned and offered his hand to Mary, "Mary, if you want to head on to the restaurant, I wanted to get something from the store."

Mary lifted an eyebrow as she stepped from the stage, but nodded, "Alright, but we need to talk, before we get back on the stage."

Nate nodded curtly, "I'll hurry," and lifted Clara from the stage before turning and jogging up the steps to the store—he wanted to get Clara a piece of nickel candy before the stage left and didn't know if there'd be time after they ate. He pulled open the door and could hear loud voices arguing inside.

"...said no, Alfred. You need to leave now." A woman's voice that sounded frantic.

"You can't marry someone else. You were supposed to marry me."

Nate stepped into the store, closing the door carefully behind him as he surveyed the scene. The young dandy was at the counter, facing a young woman. His back was to Nate, but by the woman's wide eyed and fearful look it was obvious she wasn't happy to see the dandy.

And evidently, the dandy wasn't happy about it.

The dandy... Alfred... suddenly reached across the counter and grabbed the woman's arm. "You need to talk to me about this."

She slapped his arm, "Let me go, Alfred. You're hurting me!"

Whether he was going to let go or not, Nate didn't wait to find out. He strode across the room in six quick steps and yanked Alfred around by the shoulder.

Alfred didn't hesitate; he swung a roundhouse as he turned that would have probably dropped Nate, had it landed.

But it didn't.

Nate ducked under the punch and brought up a quick right to the young dandy's ribs. Alfred lost his breath with a loud huff and slipped sideways, but Nate didn't stop to let him breathe; he jabbed a short left to his jaw that sent Alfred staggering to the side, where he fell in an unconscious heap.

Right at another man's feet.

Nate looked up as the man calmly stepped back and shook his head. "Well, I guess that's that."

Nate flushed as he noticed the white collar on the man's neck, "Um, hello... Parson..."

The Parson grinned and turned to face the woman. She was standing stiffly behind the counter, her face white as a sheet, "Are you alright?"

She shook her head in disbelief, "I don't... He..." She looked back and forth from the Parson to Nate, her eyes pleading as she was close to tears, "Why is he here?"

***** ******

The woman disappeared into the back as Nate and the Parson pulled the unconscious Alfred off to the side of the room. Then leaving Nate to watch him—on the off chance that he woke up—the Parson stepped out of the store. When he returned a few moments later, Nate helped him carry the man across the street to the jail, placing him in an empty cell. After ensuring it was locked securely, the Parson turned to face Nate, smiling apologetically. "Well, I know you're probably in a hurry, but I'll have to ask you to stay in town. The Sheriff will need to talk to you...."

Nate grew very still as a chill ran down his spine, "The Sheriff? Why would he need to speak to me?"

"Well, other than Miss Woodfield, you were the only witness of..." He gestured to the cell, "...Alfred's actions." He shook his head, "I came into the store as he swung on you, so I didn't see the initial confrontation."

Nate took a deep breath and nodded slowly, "I reckon I understand that."

The Parson motioned through the window to the other side of the street. "We don't have a hotel, but Maude has a few rooms over the restaurant that she lets out. The town will pay for the room and board while you're here."

Nate stared through the window, unsurprised to see the teamster already unloading Mary and his bags. The Parson must have signaled him somehow... He turned from the window, "Parson... I'll need to speak with my wife..."

The Parson nodded slowly, "Of course, but Mrs. Cobbins has already spoke with her and assured her you were unharmed."

Nate clenched his jaw, feeling trapped. "Yes, Sir, but all the same..."

"Alright." The Parson grinned, "Head on over to the restaurant, and I'll wait here."

Nate nodded curtly and put on his hat as he opened the door.

***** ******

William watched the young man cross the street and grinned. It was fairly obvious that the young man was on the run from something—he had about panicked at the thought of talking to James—he was just curious what that might be. Otherwise he seemed like a pretty good kid.

Chuckling, he sat down at James' desk and put his feet up.

***** ******

Nate had no sooner stepped into the restaurant when he was stopped by an older woman.

"Good afternoon, Sir. Are you looking for your young wife and girl?"

Startled, he wondered how far the story of his actions—or in this case, his confinement to town—had spread already. "Yes, Ma'am. Are they in here?"

She pointed apologetically at a narrow staircase, "I gave her a room already so she could settle in..." She leaned forward, and whispered, "That way the rest of the passengers wouldn't keep gawking at her." She nodded, "It's the first one on your right when you reach the top."

He thanked her and climbed the stairs quickly. He had barely reached the door to their room when it was pulled open—Mary had obviously heard him coming up the stairs—and faced him pale and shaking, at the open door, "What happened?" She asked frantically as she moved out of the way so he could enter. "Are you in trouble?" She sounded on the verge of tears.

Nate closed the door behind him and turned to face her. She looked like she had been crying, and her face was still puffy. "No, not yet, anyway." He looked over at the bed; Clara was already sleeping soundly on top of the quilt, "The Parson wants me to talk to the Sheriff."

If possible, her face became a shade paler than before, "Why? Because of the bank...?"

"No," He shook his head, "I was the only witness to the dandy yanking around that woman." He thought for a moment, "Well, and 'cause I was the one who stopped him."

"Still..." She sat down on the edge of the bed, "I wish you wouldn't have got involved. We needed to be far away from here."

He lifted an eyebrow and waited. He knew how she felt, but he couldn't have stood by.

She finally met his eyes, and sighed, "Oh, I know... you had to." She looked back at Clara, "Honestly, I suppose I'd be disappointed if you hadn't... but still."

He didn't know why, but her admitting that made him feel better... calmer really, about the whole situation. "Well, I need to get back across the street. I don't know how long the Sheriff will be gone, but I want to be there when he gets back. Get this over and done with."

"All right..." She opened her mouth to add something, but closed it again.

Nate stopped, hand on the knob. He could tell something more was wrong. "What is it?"

She looked down at the floor for a moment, then met his eyes, "The man... the one you called a dandy. I knew him. He's dangerous."

Nate stilled, eyes wide and stared at her. He could suddenly feel his heart beating in his temples. "You knew him?"

She nodded slowly, "I don't think he recognized me, but then again, he saw me as a child and never paid me much attention. His name is Alfred Beachem. He used to visit the girl next door from... where I lived."

Nate felt the corner of his mouth tugging in a grim smile as he remembered her recent addition of a southern accent—in her stress she had already dropped it. "Yeah, that's him... Alfred. Anyway..." He tilted his head to the side, "I agree though... I don't think he recognized you—the accent probably helped. You should be safe."

She blushed slightly, but waved her hand dismissively, "Yes, maybe in that respect... but he was one of Horace's friends." At his blank look she added, "My husband."

"Oh." He didn't know how to respond, so he just stood quietly.

"I'm just saying that everyone knew Alfred was shady..." She thought for a moment, "Everyone except my neighbors that is. The point is, Alfred knew some dangerous people."

"I see... I'll be careful."

She blew out a long breath, obviously relieved. "Alright. Hurry back."

He gave a curt nod and opened the door. He just hoped he could get back before the Sheriff did.

***** ******

Maggie knocked softly on the door before pulling it open to peer in. Catherine was sitting on the edge of her bed, her face in her hands.

"Are you alright?" Maggie offered quietly.

Catherine looked up slowly, "No, I'm not." Maggie could see the streaks on her face from the flowing tears.

Maggie sighed and stepped into the room, closing the door softly behind her, "Elizabeth told me that you didn't want to talk to anyone."

Catherine stared at her for several seconds before looking down at the floor, "That wasn't exactly what I told her..." She trailed off, "Well, maybe it was." She wiped her nose with the handkerchief she had clutched in her hand. "I guess I'm upset that *he* showed up."

"You guess you're upset...?" Maggie asked wryly, "I think it's pretty apparent." She shook her head, "And just so we are clear, by he you mean Alfred?"

Catherine nodded slowly, "Yes. I guess Elizabeth told you what happened?"

Maggie sat down on the bed next to Catherine, "Did you invite him?"

Catherine recoiled, "Oh my goodness, no. Why would you ask that?"

Maggie shrugged, "If it was Alfred's choice to show up here, then it's no fault of yours. And it doesn't look like it was a good choice on his part, but he is the one that will have to deal with those consequences."

Catherine groaned softly and buried her face in her hands, "The good Lord knows he deserves consequences, but why did it have to involve me?" Her body shook with sudden sobs, "I'm supposed to marry James in a little over a week. Why is God doing this to me?"

Maggie sighed and reached over, patting Catherine's arm, "I'm sure that somewhere in this, God has a reason for allowing Alfred to show up."

"A reason?" Catherine looked up, shaking her head in disgust, "What good could possibly come from him showing up right before my wedding?"

"Honestly, I don't know." She shrugged, "What I do know is that every time that I've had a major disappointment in my life, God was using it to show me something."

Catherine huffed sarcastically, "Yes, to show me I was a foolish little girl. That I foolishly wasted two years of my life on him."

Maggie shook her head, "No... I mean, I understand what you are saying, but God doesn't take our failures and rub them in our faces." She chuckled softly, "Well, He will if that's what it takes to get our attention, but after we choose the right path—the path that pleases Him—He doesn't browbeat us for our mistakes." She met Catherine's eyes, "Think of it like this; what if you had married Alfred earlier? Then you'd be stuck in a marriage with a known criminal, right?"

Catherine nodded mutely.

Maggie continued, "And, if you had realized earlier on that Alfred wasn't a good man, you may have married someone else, right?"

Catherine nodded again, "I suppose that's true."

"If either of those had happened, then you would have never met James, and would never have the opportunity for a happy life with him, right?"

Catherine shrugged, "I've never thought of it like that."

"We usually don't. We prefer to sit around in self-pity. Trust me, I know."

Catherine raised an eyebrow, "You know?"

Maggie shook her head, "You think I've lived my life without disappointments, especially in the area of love? I had a beau in New York. He was a Doctor." She could feel her jaw tighten just mentioning it—it still hurt to think about, "He was just fine when I was a nurse, and when I started medical school, he was... tolerant." She closed her eyes, remembering the last time she had spoken with him, "Then one day, right before I graduated, he explained to me how embarrassing it was for him that I was trying to be a doctor. He'd humored me long enough, but I needed to quit and accept my station in life." She tried to keep the bitterness out of her tone, but it was hard. She met Catherine's eyes, "When I refused, he broke off our engagement and married one of my friends three weeks later."

Catherine stared, obviously shocked. "Oh, my—I'm so sorry."

Maggie waved a hand dismissively, "No apology needed. I'm not looking for pity; I just want you to understand that sometimes these things are for the best. God used that to bring me here. Now, I'm looking to see what that was for."

Catherine nodded slowly, "I can understand that." She blew out a long breath, "But why did God let him get on a stage and come all the way out here, now?"

"Like I said, I honestly don't know. God doesn't always list His reasons. It might even be the devil testing you, to see if you'd change your mind and run back to Alfred."

"I would never do that."

Maggie lifted an eyebrow, "Are you sure? I mean, what if it turned out that he was actually innocent of the crimes that they arrested him for? That was why you really broke it off with him, right."

Catherine frowned, "Do you think he is?"

Maggie shrugged, "He's out for some reason, but does it matter?"

Catherine stared at the floor for a full minute before answering, "No, it doesn't."

Relieved, Maggie tilted her head, "Why not?"

Catherine blew out a breath, "It wasn't until I came West that I began to see how badly he treated me. It was like he expected me to be a decoration for him and that was all. He would..." She trailed off, "No, now I would never consider it, even if I didn't love James."

Maggie nodded, "Then, why are you up here crying about it?"

***** ******

TEN

James flopped open the door to the jail and stepped in, pausing when he saw the Parson and another man standing by his desk. "Hello Parson, how can I help y'all?"

Parson William had a serious look on his face, "James, I want you to meet Nate... he was a passenger on the last stage through."

The young man, Nate, stepped forward and offered his hand, "Sir, good to meet you."

James shook his hand, appreciating the firm grip. "Likewise. Why aren't you still on the stage?" He looked from Nate to Parson William, not liking the serious look on the Parson's face. "Somethin' happen?"

Parson William gestured with his thumb to the cells in the back. "Well, we have a visitor back there... he came to see a woman in town. Tried to hurt her from what I understood."

"Who...?" His mind raced through the options and felt his jaw tighten suddenly, "Catherine? Was it Alfred?"

Parson William nodded slowly, "Yes, it was."

His face tight with anger, James started to turn back toward the door, "Is she all right?"

"Hold up, James." Parson Williams' voice stopped him. "She's upset, but not hurt. Elizabeth and Doc Maggie are with her, and that's what she needs right now."

"Harumph!" James tapped his foot nervously. Part of him was irritated—he wasn't sure what the other part felt quite yet. "You think I should go back there and deal with him?" A lot of towns he'd been through out west would've hung a man for layin' hands on a woman. He didn't see why Cobbinsville had to be different.

Parson William smiled grimly and nodded toward the cells. "You're the Sheriff... I'd say you'll eventually have to talk to him, but right now he's still unconscious."

James lifted an eyebrow, "How'd that..." His eyes tracked to Nate, who stood quietly by. "You?"

The young man dipped his head slightly, "Yes, Sir."

James grinned widely, immediately deciding to like the young man. "Thanks."

Parson William cleared his throat. "Well, James, something for you to think about. Apparently, Alfred was telling the other passengers on the stage he was coming out here to get married. I would guess he meant Catherine..." He trailed off with a shrug.

James recoiled in surprise, "What?"

"That's what he told us on the stage," Nate offered quietly. "And when I came into the store, he was telling her that she couldn't marry..." he shrugged apologetically, "I suppose he meant you Sheriff. Anyway, he was saying that she was supposed to marry him."

"Marry him?" James shook his head and looked at Parson William. "She broke it off with him months ago. Didn't Catherine say he was supposed to be in jail?"

Parson William leaned against the desk, "Yes. Just so you know, I told Ray to send a telegram to Philadelphia once they made it to Dana. Maybe check with the Marshal as well and see what he had to say." He grinned, "Plus, we can ask him when he wakes up."

James nodded, "Sounds good, if he'll tell the truth."

"Then that's our plan." Parson William picked up his hat, "I'll head over and check on Catherine and let them know you'll be by in a bit."

"Ok, Parson. I appreciate that."

Parson William left, and the door had just shut with a loud bang when the young man cleared his throat, "Sheriff... how long will you need us to stay in town?"

James tilted his head to the side, "I'm not exactly certain yet. Next stage won't be 'til Monday... we won't hear anything until then. The town'll pay for your room and meals, but there's nothing I can do about the inconvenience."

Nate shook his head slowly, "I understand, I s'pose. We're just a tad antsy to get moving."

"We?" James remembered the young man had used a plural earlier as well.

"My wife and daughter. We're headed to California."

"Ah, I see. Well, beautiful country out that way." James grinned, "Not as pretty as here though." He sat down at his desk, "Wish I could get you moving on a bit quicker, but I reckon I should make sure this is done right. I don't want to be accused of bias."

"Parson mentioned you were 'bout to get hitched to the young lady in the store," Nate grinned, "I can see why that would cause a little concern."

"Yeah, there is that." James sighed, tapping the desk. "Well, if'n you get bored waiting I might scare up someone who could use an extra hand for a day or two, long as you're here. Be some extra cash, anyway."

Nate grinned widely, "I'd be obliged, Sheriff. That room looks mighty small for the three of us."

James stood suddenly, picking up his hat from the desk, "Well, I waited long enough. I'll walk you back over to the restaurant and head over to see Catherine."

***** ******

James paused at the doorway to the setting room. Catherine was in a chair on the far side, facing a bright painting of a smiling young girl at a large piano.

He watched her for several seconds, not wanting to disturb her, but finally offered softly, "Are you doin' alright?"

Catherine turned sharply, her face immediately lighting up. "James!" She stood quickly and crossed the room. "I am so sorry..."

James tilted his head, confused. "What for?"

Catherine stopped a few feet away, and he couldn't tell if she was sad, mad, or confused. "For Alfred coming. I am so..." Tears started to well at the corner of her eyes, and she looked down at the floor.

"Whoa there." James stepped forward, taking her hand. "You didn't ask him to come. He just came on his own. That's not your fault."

She met his eyes, and he could see the pain and embarrassment she felt. "I had told him I never wanted to see him again."

He patted her hand, "See, there ya go. He's just thick headed." He gestured to the chair, "I'm just glad you weren't hurt."

Catherine smiled bitterly as she took a seat on the chair, "Well, my self-respect took a bit of a nosedive, but the Parson was there, and some man from the stage."

"I know, they told me about it." He sat in the chair across from her, leaning forward slightly. "Don't you worry about him. We've already sent word to the Marshal—since the last thing we heard about Alfred was that he was in jail, we'll need to see if'n he's wanted anywhere."

Catherine nodded slowly, "That's probably a good idea."

"Either way, he'll leave here by himself—whether in leg irons or not." He grinned broadly, "So there's nothing to worry yourself about."

"Thanks, James." Her body visibly relaxed, and she blew out a deep breath, "I was just worried you would be upset with me... Maggie told me I was being silly, but still." She gave a small smile, "And I'll bet she'll be thrilled that the Marshal will be on the way... but, enough of that. Let's forget about Alfred and talk about us. How is work coming at the house?"

James grinned at her desire to change the subject. "It's gettin' close. Unfortunately, Widow Johnson had let some things get in pretty rough shape over the years." He always tried to be vague, hoping to hide the full extent of repairs the house needed. The house was just outside of town, and until recently had been the home of an old widow woman who'd taken a liking to Catherine and left it to her when she passed. "I had to replace the floor in the kitchen, and a few other things, but Earl's been coming in here and there to help."

Catherine hid her mouth and giggled, "More *here* than there... here meaning Maude's restaurant. I think he's taken with her."

James tilted his head to the side, "So, that's why he's always needing to run into town... I thought they were looking at each other funny, but I didn't know the scoundrel was..." He trailed off, laughing. "Well, anyway, it is going well." He looked at the clock, "Well, darlin' I better go. Much as I hate to bring him up, I do have a prisoner at the jail that I best tend to." His jaw tightened as the mirth dropped from her face like a curtain. Standing quickly, he grabbed his hat. "But, don't worry. Just another week, and we'll be married, and this will be a memory."

Catherine stood and quietly walked him to the door. "Ok..." She thought for a moment, "I might take a break though... with him here it just..." She trailed off for a moment, "I was thinking about having Ted drive me out to see Anna and the twins. I was thinking I could stay over and ride back in with them for Church Sunday."

James nodded slowly, "I understand. No problem." He grinned, "Just make sure you do come back now. We're getting married next weekend, so don't try to skip out."

"I won't, James..." She shook her head, "But, you just be careful. I couldn't stand to see you get hurt."

"Yes'm. I certainly will."

As he left the house and started walking back to the jail, he found himself chuckling. He really didn't think he'd have to worry about getting hurt by Alfred—the only times he had been hurt in the last few months had been by her.

***** ******

Alfred started banging as soon as James stepped through the door of the jail.

"I demand to be let out of this cell."

James took a deep breath and reminded himself that he couldn't shoot Alfred... well, yet anyway. He faced the red-faced man and kept his face neutral. "Sir, you have been placed under arrest for assaulting a woman and attempting to assault another man. You aren't going anywhere right now."

Alfred's face grew an extra shade darker red. "Assaulting a woman? I did not assault a woman!"

"I have the sworn testimony of two witnesses, both of which you attempted to..."

"Are you talking about the man who hit me?" Alfred's voice rose a few octaves as he spoke, obviously flustered. "That man grabbed me, and I was trying to defend myself."

James blew out a long breath, trying to be patient. "The young man in question, as seen by witnesses, was preventing the continued assault of a woman." Alfred started to interrupt, but James cut him off with a curt gesture, "Let me tell you something, Alfred. You are no longer back East. Out here, they take assaulting a woman seriously. In some places, they'll hang a man for less." He jerked a thumb toward the door, "I wouldn't test this town."

Alfred recoiled and took a few steps back. "Hang?" He shook his head, "I was just speaking to her. She is my fiancé."

James scratched his finger on the butt of his pistol—a nervous habit he had when he really wanted to shoot someone. "Alfred, Catherine specifically asked you to never see her again." He shook his head, "I'm not sure what you hoped to gain by coming west, but Catherine was already finished with you—and for that matter, she is also spoken for." With a final shake of his head, he turned and stepped back out of the jail.

***** ******

William spread his face into a wide grin when James stepped out on the porch. He could tell James wasn't happy. "Have a seat, James."

James started and glanced over, surprise lighting his features. "Sorry, Parson. Didn't notice you were there." He sat down, still obviously agitated. "I figured you'd be heading back to the house by now. What's going on?"

"You tell me." He jerked a thumb back toward the jail. "He quieted down pretty quick."

165

James scratched the back of his neck, "Well, I may have mentioned what usually happens to men who mistreat womenfolk out here."

William chuckled, "Threatened to hang him, eh?"

"No...not exactly." James tilted his head, "Ok, I may have mentioned it was an option."

"Right." William leaned back in his chair, enjoying the slight breeze. "Something I wanted you to remember, James—God has a plan for everything, whether we realize it or not. He brought Alfred here for something... for some reason. We just might not be aware of why yet."

James leaned back in his chair and grunted, "I dunno Parson. I guess I'd never really thought of that."

William nodded slowly, "Most of us don't. We only see what we want." He glanced sideways, "How was Catherine?"

James shrugged absently, "She was doin' alright. Had a good talk with Doc Maggie... She didn't say, but I reckon that helped her more'n I could've."

William nodded slowly, gesturing toward the store across the street. "You know, sometimes people have problems closing off their past—it's possible that God brought him here to prove to her once and for all that she didn't need or want Alfred." He paused for a moment and added, "God moves in strange ways sometimes... you take that boy, Nate. I believe God brought that boy into town for something as well. You watch him... he's skittish, like he's running from something."

James gave a sideways grin, "He is a tad twitchy, but he comes off as a good kid. Probably did something dumb at some point, but I'm not too worried." He paused for a moment and added, "You think I should check him out?"

William gestured absently, "If you want, but I don't think it's necessary." He grinned, "He's not dangerous... 'cept to Alfred I suppose, and that's one thing that gives me a good feeling about him." He chuckled softly, "You should've seen that boy lay Alfred out... was a time we could've done it, but nowadays we'd be hurting from the effort. That's what age is doing to us."

James huffed out a quiet laugh, "Now you're starting to sound like Earl. Next thing you'll be complaining about your rheumatiz' and bad back. Then—Katie bar the door, you'll be planning your own funeral."

They shared another laugh and fell silent. A gust of wind stirred up a dust devil in the middle of the street, and William watched it dance and dissipate. He looked off to his left; he could see dark clouds building up in the distance. Another storm brewing.

And in the back of his mind, he knew it was a sign of things to come.

***** ******

ELEVEN

Anna Stone pulled her scarf up as she stepped out onto the porch, shading her eyes with her hand to see the wagon pulling into the yard. She had been dozing by the window when the sound of a wagon rolling down the trail woke her. She had jumped up and looked out the window to see a wagon clearing the trees as her husband, William, rode past on his horse toward the barn.

The wagon pulled up on the hard-packed dirt in front of the house. Ted Cobbins, who ran the store in town, and his sister in law Catherine were the only passengers—Anna knew this wasn't a social call—she knew something must be wrong, but she kept the smile on her face.

Without waiting for her brother in law to help her, Catherine stepped easily off the wagon and onto the ground.

"Catherine!" Anna called to the young woman, "I'm glad you've come."

"Hello, Miss Anna." Catherine crossed the yard and stepped onto the porch, embracing Anna in a tight hug. "How are the twins?"

"Sleeping, thankfully. Although..." She gestured to the barn, "As soon as they realize their Pa is home, they'll be awake." She straightened her scarf to cover the side of her face. She had been burned severely several years before, and even though William didn't like her to, she preferred to wear it when she was around other people. "Now, why don't you tell me why you're here, because I know you didn't ride all this way just to see the twins."

Catherine nodded slowly, looking back as her brother in law pulled a small bag from the wagon, and then turned back, "Alfred came to town." Even though she spoke quietly, Anna could hear the pain and stress in her voice.

Anna recoiled in surprise, "Alfred? Came here?" She turned to the door, "Come inside and we'll talk. William will get your bag when he's done."

Anna's mind was racing as they moved into the main room of the house. Catherine had told her all about her relationship with Alfred when she had become interested in James. From what Catherine had told her, Alfred was a horrible person; he had emotionally abused her throughout their relationship, and she hadn't seen it until he had been arrested for stealing. Catherine had broken off the relationship and came west to stay with her sister Elizabeth.

But now Alfred had followed her here? Why? She shook off the thought and turned to Catherine with a smile, "Would you like some tea?"

Catherine shook her head, "Maybe some water." She watched as Anna poured her a glass from a short pitcher and sat heavily in a chair before taking a long drink. She sighed in satisfaction as she set the glass down "Thanks...it's a long ride out to your house."

Anna sat in the chair across from Catherine and grabbed her teacup from the small table where she had sat it earlier. It had grown cool, but she didn't want to leave Catherine to warm it up. "Perhaps that is a good thing. Does Alfred know you came here?"

"No, I'm not even certain he was conscious when I left."

Anna leaned forward, "This story is sounding more interesting by the minute." She supposed that Catherine was as clumsy with Alfred as she had been with James. It hadn't been that long ago that she'd split James' head open with her suitcase, broken his nose with a door, and shot him in the leg. "What did you do to him?"

Catherine gasped sharply, "I..." She trailed off with a weak smile. "Oh, no... it wasn't me." She tilted her head slightly, "Though, I wish it had been."

Anna sat, spellbound as Catherine recounted the entire story of Alfred's arrival. She could not believe so much had happened in so little time. It was just a few days ago William had told her about an issue with some other men harassing Catherine in the store. And now this? She clucked her tongue, "I am so sorry, Catherine."

Catherine sighed loudly, sitting back in her chair. "I've just been struggling lately with fear and doubt, and it seemed like things were just getting worse." She shook her head, "So I prayed, and I asked God to help me through this, help me to stop feeling like this all the time." She shook her head sadly, "And now this." She blew out a long breath, "I mean, I talked with Doc Maggie earlier, and she talked about how God might be using this to show me something... what she told me made sense—I even felt better for a little while—but now I'm just..." She trailed off with a wave of her hand, obviously close to tears.

Anna leaned back and took another sip of her tea, thinking hard before she spoke. Catherine was going through a rough time, that was certain, but she didn't want to pander to a sense of helplessness and self-pity. "Catherine..." She chose her words carefully, "The problem you are having right now isn't with Alfred." She paused at Catherine's surprised look, then continued, "It isn't even with fear." She gestured with her cup, "The problem you are having is with your perspective."

Catherine drew back, obviously confused, "My what?"

Anna leaned over and set her cup on the table, picking up a small notebook and pencil she used for her devotions. "Look at this word." She printed a single word, 'emphasis' on the paper. "How do you pronounce this word?"

Catherine leaned in close, studying the word, "Emphasis... **EM**-fa-sis. Right?"

"Yes... but what if you stress the second syllable, instead of the first? It becomes em-**FA**-sis, right?"

Catherine smiled hesitantly and leaned back, "I suppose, but what does that have to do with me?"

"Would you recognize it if someone pronounced it like that?"

Catherine shrugged, "Well, probably not... maybe. Why?"

Anna sat the pad down, picking her cup back up. "Simply this; we spend too much of our time with our focus on the wrong things. We emphasize the wrong things in our lives—just like this word—when you do that, it messes things up to where God's order is unrecognizable. God has a plan for our lives, His love and protection are with us constantly, but when we focus on the wrong things—when we emphasize the wrong syllables of our lives—we no longer see God's hand, and our faith struggles as a result." She gestured with her cup again, "Catherine, God has seen you through a lot in your life, and has brought you here for a purpose, kept you safe through several horrible situations—and you are ignoring all of that to emphasize the negative."

Catherine sat very still for several seconds before responding, "I never really..." She trailed off for a moment, shaking her head, "I was so caught up in the events, that I guess I missed how God was carrying me through it."

Anna smiled sadly, "That's easy for all of us to do." She reached up a touched her scarf, "For too many years I hid from everyone because of my personal pain... it wasn't until William came that I realized that God had been with me through all of those trials." She took a sip of her tea, "And if you step back, I'm sure you can see that now."

Catherine huffed out a quiet laugh, "Well, I suppose that it was James that got me here..." She leaned forward and spoke in a mock whisper, "Probably not a good idea to let him know. It'll go to his head."

They shared a laugh, which elicited a cry from one of the twins in the other room, which in turn started the second one crying as well. Anna stood with a groan, "Well, it looks like nap time is over."

***** ******

TWELVE

"Nate!"

Nate snapped awake and reached for his pistol, scanning the room from his spot on the floor. Mary was sitting up on the bed, her eyes wide with fear.

He blinked twice before finding his voice, "What's going on?"

"Clara won't wake up. She's burning with fever!"

Nate stood quickly, almost falling as his feet got tangled in his bedroll, "What should I do?" He looked around, feeling helpless. He'd never dealt with a sick child before. He couldn't even remember being sick as a boy.

She waved impatiently at the door, "Get a doctor!"

"What?" He started to kick his bedroll to the side, but then paused suddenly.

"What are you doing?" Mary's voice had risen to a shrill level of panic.

"I'm going." He gathered the bedroll up quickly and dropped it on the chair. He didn't want the Doctor to ask questions. He stepped out of the room and moved quickly down the steps. He had no idea who he was looking for, or where to find a doctor—his first thought was to head for the Sheriff.

"What's wrong?" A woman's clear voice called out behind him.

Nate stopped near the bottom of the steps, turning to find a tall woman at the top tying a robe around her waist. "I need a doctor."

"Where?" She motioned behind her, "That room? I'm going." She immediately disappeared in a flurry of white fabric.

Confused, Nate turned and headed for the door. He supposed that woman could help while he went and got the Sheriff.

He crossed the street quickly and pounded on the jail door. "Sheriff!"

What seems like an eternity later, the Sheriff opened the door, pistol in hand. He looked at Nate, then glanced side to side at the street. "What's going on?"

Nate jerked his thumb toward the restaurant, "Clara's sick. My... daughter. I need a doctor."

The Sheriff opened the door wide and stepped out. "Doc Maggie's stayin' up there." He pulled the door shut behind him as a voice in the back started yelling something about sleep. "Did you ask her?"

Nate shook his head, confused. "Her? A woman doctor?" He jumped down from the porch and started back across the street with the Sheriff following close behind him. "There was a tall yellow haired woman..."

"Yep." The Sheriff answered curtly, "She's good... and probably better than Doc Merten for a little girl anyway."

By the time they made it up to the room, Maude—the woman who ran the place—was standing outside the doorway with her arm around Mary's shoulders. Nate slowed as he neared them, fearing the worst. "Is she..."

"Doc Maggie's in with her now, trying to cool her down." Maude offered quietly. "I'm sure she'll be fine. You just head on downstairs and leave this to us."

Nate, knowing a dismissal when he heard one, took her advice immediately and went back down the steps to the restaurant. The low lamps gave off a dull glow, making it difficult to see. He turned one lamp up, blinking at the bright light, and sat in a nearby chair to wait.

He felt horrible—and partly to blame for the girl's condition. He was certain it was all the time on the trail, all those cool evenings under the stars that had made the little girl sick. He just hoped she would get by.

He felt like this would be a good time to pray but couldn't see God wanting to hear from him right then.

Instead, he sat staring at the wall, hoping that Clara made it through the night.

***** ******

By the time the sun came up, Clara's fever had come down slightly, but she was still struggling to breathe. The Sheriff had left to check on his houseguest, and Nate had been left alone in the restaurant until Maude came downstairs to start working in the kitchen.

"Fever's rough on a little girl."

Nate looked up from his coffee. The Sheriff had come back in the room and was standing a few feet away. "Yes, Sir. I believe so."

"Prayin' for her."

"I appreciate that." He gestured to the seat across from him, "Have a seat." He waved Maude over as the Sheriff sat down, gesturing for another cup of coffee. It was difficult to express his appreciation for the man's prayers... considering how certain he was that God wasn't interested in his right then.

"If'n you need some rest, there's a bunk over at the jail you can use." He grinned, "Other fellas settled down now."

"No, I'm good. Thanks." Nate grimaced slightly at the offer; he had no interest in being near the jail, just in case. For all he knew, he might look up and see his face on a wanted poster.

"Well, it's an open invite." Maude arrived with coffee for the Sheriff, and he sipped lightly. "So, any specific reason you're headin' for California?"

Nate stiffened, but still tried to answer nonchalantly, "Change of scenery. We knew some people that went that way. Sounded like a good place for a start."

The Sheriff looked him over, "Yeah, you're young enough to need a start." He chuckled, "Old feller like me has to call it 'starting over.'"

They shared a quiet laugh, and Nate shook his head, "Well, Sheriff, I really don't think you're to the 'old feller' level quite yet." He grinned, gesturing with his cup, "You ain't too much older than me, I think."

"Heh, old enough." He leaned forward, "You can call me James... by the way. Sheriff sounds like I'm about to arrest someone."

Nate smiled, hoping that wasn't going to be the case. "Sure, James." He took another sip of coffee, "You're getting married soon, right? To the woman from the store?"

"Sure am." James sat up a little straighter, obviously proud, "Prettiest thing in Wyoming, and she chose me." He paused, "Not to say your'n is ugly or anything..."

Nate waved dismissively, "No offense taken. I'm glad you two are happy."

James tilted his head to the side, "How old are you anyway? You two seem awful young to have..."

He was interrupted as Doc Maggie came down the steps. They both stood; Nate was halfway between thankfulness the Sheriff's question got derailed, and fear over what the Doc was going to tell them.

"She's resting right now. The fever is down some, but she is struggling to breathe." She gestured to the door, "I was going to head over to the store and get a few things, but you can go on up if you'd like."

Nate nodded, "Thank you." As she left the room, he glanced over at the Sheriff, "Well, Sheriff... James, I'm gonna run up and check on them really quick."

James sat down and picked up his cup, "Well, yer little girl will likely be bedridden for a few days at least. I told you I'd get you some work, but I don't think you'd want to get too far from town— 'specially with the little girl sick." He shrugged apologetically, "If you want, I have some work yet to do on the house afore the wedding—it's just outside of town... not too far. I can pay yeh to help out there."

"Alright," Nate offered appreciatively, "I'll get with you after a bit."

"I'm gonna finish my coffee, then I'll be back across the street."

Nate gave a final wave as he mounted the steps. He wouldn't mind doing some work if they were going to be in town for long, but he would have to be very careful how any conversations went.

***** ******

Marshal Lucas Sterling stepped down from his horse and looked around the small town as he tied the reins to the short rail in front of the Sheriff's office. It didn't look much different than when he left; of course, that *had* only been a few weeks ago.

He could hear thunder in the distance; the chill in the air told him that it would probably rain pretty soon.

A soft voice interrupted his reverie, "Well, Marshal. I was wondering when you were going to come back this way."

Lucas smiled at the familiar voice and turned, "Maggie. Good to see you." He smiled appreciatively; she had stepped out of the store with a small brown package in her hand, looking beautiful, even in the plain dress she was wearing.

"Did you come for the wedding?" Maggie shook her head, "No, it's too early for that. I guess you're here on business... Probably came for that man Alfred."

He grinned at her directness, "Well, I do have to take that young man back to the railroad when the stage comes Monday, but then I'll be coming back for the wedding." He gestured to the package, "Whatcha got there? Rheumatiz medicine for someone?"

"No," She shook her head, "Its medicine for a sick little girl." She gestured to the hotel, "Daughter of the man who stopped Alfred from hurting Catherine, matter of fact. She took sick late last night."

"Awww, that's sad. But..." Lucas grinned broadly, "...I suppose it was fortuitous that they had stopped here. Best Doc in the state to tend to her."

Maggie blushed, "Oh, stop it, Lucas."

"Brought me back from the brink." And he wasn't kidding when he said that. Just a few short months ago he had been riding across the plains during an investigation and had ended up snake bit in the middle of nowhere. His horse had brought him to town half dead, and she had tended him back to health. "Plus," He added with a grin, "You were awful good company."

"Now, that'll be enough of that smooth talking from you." She waved at the restaurant, "The Sheriff was in the restaurant a few minutes ago, and I can't imagine him being done yet."

"Well," Lucas grinned, "I suppose that means I'll get to escort you back that direction." He offered his arm, "Ma'am...?"

Maggie took his arm, and they walked down the short walk to the restaurant. They had barely stepped through the door when James called from a nearby table, "Well, hello there Marshal Sterling. Looks like you made it without gettin' bit this time." He chuckled at his own joke as he stood and crossed the room, offering his hand.

They shook briefly, "Good to see you as well, James. Busy week?"

James rubbed his face with his hand, "It was already busy, this fool has made it worse." He gestured to the table behind him, "You ate yet?"

"I left out early so I could make it down." He gave a sideways glance at Maggie, "Hoping for some visiting time before I left on the stage Monday."

That elicited a blush from Maggie, who waved her package, "Well, visiting will have to wait for later. I have a sick little girl upstairs. I'll catch up with you later, Lucas."

She climbed the stairs quickly, disappearing from sight. Lucas watched her go, then turned back to James. "Well, I have a few people to talk to." He tilted his head, "How is Catherine doing? Do you think she'll be ok to talk about what happened?"

James nodded thoughtfully, "I think so, 'cept she went out to the Parson's house to spend time with Miss Anna. She didn't want to be in the same town with Alfred."

Lucas snorted a laugh, "Well, I can see that... and the Parson's there as well. That leaves the young man with a sick daughter, and Alfred." At James' nod, he shook his head, "I'll talk to him tomorrow maybe. Don't want too much on him."

James shook his head, "Nah, kid seems pretty solid. I don't think it'll be a problem."

"Well, that may be... but right now I think I'll talk to Alfred. I'd rather get this over and done with, and I'll want you there."

James lifted an eyebrow but didn't ask questions. He started toward the door, "All right then, let's head over."

It was a short trip across the street. James held the door open for Lucas, "Straight through to the back."

"Thanks." As they walked to the back, Lucas pulled the paperwork from the satchel he carried.

There was only one cell occupied; the man inside was sour looking enough, but he was sporting a large purple bruise along his jawline that made him look sickly as well. He glared at James briefly before turning to him with a questioning look.

Lucas cleared his throat, "Hello, Sir. Are you Alfred Perceval Beachem, lately of Philadelphia, Pennsylvania?"

The man stood, "Yes, I am. May I ask who you are, sir?" Alfred's attempt at civility came off more as sarcasm. Lucas held up the warrant, "This was signed by the Territorial Judge and is for your arrest and transportation back to Pennsylvania. You are wanted for..." He turned it back around so he could read it, "Let's see, larceny, theft, burglary, escaping custody, and the final one is..." he looked up, "Murder."

"Murder?" Alfred recoiled as if he'd been slapped, "Sir, you have the wrong man. I did not kill anyone."

Lucas sighed loudly, "You may not have meant to, but you did. There was a guard in the sewer that attempted to stop your escape." He looked back down at the paper, "I believe you knocked him unconscious."

Alfred nodded frantically, "Yes, that is all I did. Knocked him unconscious."

Lucas shook his head, "He went down face first in water. By the time they found him, he had drowned." He folded the warrant, "He had a wife and three children to support."

Alfred backed up a few steps and sat down hard on the cot, "But, they can't charge me with murder for that. It was an accident."

"Well, the law specifically states that when in commission of a felony; which escape from custody and assaulting an officer would both apply, any death that results from that felonious act will be considered murder." Lucas shook his head, "If you wouldn't have tried to escape, then that man would have gone home to his family. But you'll have an opportunity to plead that case in court." He pulled his watch from his vest pocket and glanced at it. "We'll be leaving on the next stage to catch the train east... day after tomorrow. I'd get some rest and think about what you've done."

He turned on his heel and walked back out of the cell area, straight out the front door of the building with James on his heels. He stopped to face James. "Well, that's done."

"That was a tad unexpected... for me and him."

Lucas chuckled, "Well, it was a lot easier to explain it once. Now I'll let him sit and stew on it." He could hear Alfred yelling for them both to come back, even halfway across the street. "I'm not here to argue—I'm not the judge or jury—I'm just here to give him the charge and transport him."

James chuckled softly as they reached the Marshal's horse, "I ain't got an issue with that at all. Long as you take him when you leave, I don't care how or where he goes." He blew out a soft whistle, "Looks like it might be straight into a noose though."

"Probably will be." He shook his head and gestured to his horse. "But, that's not my concern. I was going to talk to the Parson tomorrow, but with Maggie tied up, I think I'll ride out to the Parson's house. I can speak to him and Catherine at the same time." He untied the reins and swung up onto the horse.

James grunted, "Well, you ride safe. Smells like a storm moving in."

Lucas nodded curtly, "Gotcha. Back after a bit." And with that, rode quickly out of town.

***** ******

It was moving toward evening when the woman Doctor stopped downstairs to tell him she was going to freshen up and get a bite to eat. Nate stood, dropping a dime on the table before climbing the stairs to check on Clara. Mary looked up when he opened the door.

"Are you alright?" He stepped in, closing the door behind himself.

Mary nodded, "I'm fine." She gestured to Clara, "Her temperature is still down, but her breathing..." She trailed off with a sigh.

Nate nodded; he could hear the small girl's ragged breathing from his spot by the door.

Mary jumped as lightning flashed right outside the window, followed immediately by a crack of thunder that shook the entire building and rattled the window for several seconds.

Nate stepped across the room and glanced out of the window. The rain was just starting to fall, but as he watched it turned into a sudden deluge. The rain looked like a steel curtain being drawn across the sky; within seconds he lost sight of the ugly jail, even though it was right across the street. "Looks pretty bad out there."

"I'm just thankful we aren't still out on the plain..." Mary offered quietly. "I can't imagine trying to find shelter from this."

Nate nodded slowly and turned from the window. With the Doc gone, he finally had a chance to speak with Mary alone for a few minutes—he'd been looking forward to it all day long—but, now that he had the chance, he didn't know how to start. He watched her for several seconds, amazed at how pretty she looked despite being completely worn out. Her face was tight as she watched Clara, and the bags under her eyes were proof she hadn't had any rest... "You look tired." He offered lamely.

She looked up, a thin smile on her face, "Why thank you, Nate."

"I didn't mean you didn't look nice." He bit his lip, knowing that had sounded dumb. "I mean you look pretty, but tired." At her amused look he shook his head, "Anyway, Miss Maude, the woman running the place, offered me another room whilst Clara's sick. That way she could have the bed in here."

Mary gave a soft smile, "That was nice of her."

"Yeah, well, I was thinking... you look exhausted. If you want, you can go get some rest for a bit, and I can sit with Clara."

Mary lifted an eyebrow at the offer but shook her head, "No, I'll be fine. You go ahead."

Nate's jaw tightened, but he nodded; he didn't bother telling her, but it would be a cold day where the booger man lived before he laid down in a bed in the middle of the afternoon while she sat up with her sick daughter.... sister... whatever. "Maybe later. How are things going with the Doc?"

Mary's face lit up, "Oh, she is so nice. I don't know what we would have done without her."

"Lucky she was here." He picked up the candlestick from the small stand by the window, turning it in his fingers. "Sheriff stopped in a few times today." He spoke casually, not wanting to alarm Mary. "Wanted us to know they were prayin' for Clara. He seems like a friendly guy."

Mary clucked her tongue, "Well, he's probably feeling well within your debt for punching that yahoo messing with his fiancé." She huffed out a brief laugh, "Probably not a bad thing."

"That's true." Nate grinned, "But I'd still rather be on the trail heading west." He hooked a thumb toward the window, "I keep getting a picture in my mind of the good Sheriff writing his fiancé some love poem on a piece of paper, and when he turns it over, it's my wanted poster."

Mary laughed aloud, "Oh my soul, Nate. That's awful."

"I reckon." He scratched the back of his head, "You sure there's nothing I could do for you?"

Mary smiled weakly, "Well, if you want to, you can sit with me until the Doc get back." She met his eyes, and he could see the hopeful look. "We could just talk... to keep me awake."

"Yes, Ma'am. No problem." He sat easily in the chair but was worried. Despite all the time they had spent together, he had no idea what to talk about.

***** ******

The rest of Friday passed quickly, despite the tedium. Nate sat in the restaurant drinking coffee and playing checkers with Maude, occasionally going upstairs to check on Mary and Clara. It eventually stopped raining, but it was too wet to go out—even if he would have had someplace to go.

But by early evening, he was exhausted and bored. He'd been going upstairs throughout the afternoon to get updates on Clara, but there wasn't much to do otherwise.

When the Sheriff finally came back in, he'd been quietly shuffling a deck of cards at one of the tables in the restaurant. As he finished shuffling, he would deal out a hand, gather them up and began shuffling once more.

James sat down at the table and watched him for a few minutes. "You gonna play with those?"

Nate shook his head as he dealt out a hand. "No, Sir." He gathered the cards and started shuffling again. "My Ma'd roll over in her grave if she saw me playing cards."

James huffed out a laugh, "Sounds like my Ma." He gestured to the cards, "You seem pretty handy with them."

"Dexterity. Keeps my fingers loose and nimble." Nate smiled, "Never played a game in my life though. Worked on the docks with a gambler who swore by learnin' to shuffle. Said it kept him alive."

"Alive?" James lifted an eyebrow, "If he did it for a living, why was he working at the docks?"

Nate laughed, "Well, he was a horrible gambler and always broke. That's why he was working on the docks with me." He shuffled a few more times, "There was a few times he tried to cheat, he got caught and needed a gun pretty quick...." He shuffled once more and dealt out a hand, "Nimble fingers saved his life."

James grunted, "Well, I agree with both our Ma's anyway. Stay away from the cards, and you might not need a gun."

Nate paused, eyeing the Sheriff questioningly, "Seems to me like you've seen a fair bit of gun play without the cards." That morning over coffee, Maude had told him about a shootout a few weeks before in which the Sheriff almost lost his life.

"Well, that's the danger of the job is what that is." Grinning, James took a long sip of his coffee, "'sides, I'm a professional."

"A professional?" Nate chuckled as he picked up the cards, "Well, I s'pose that's true, but it seems like it'd be safer to not be a professional. Less chance of getting shot."

"Not exactly, but close." James shook his head, "I was deputy in a town out west, New Mexico territory. I saw quite a few gunfights when the only people hit were on the sidelines." He clucked his tongue, "Never could understand why anyone thought watching two men shoot each other was sport."

"No... I mean, I guess there were times..." Nate straightened the deck and set it to the side, "...times I knew one of the men and wanted to see if his draw matched his brag—but, I've seen men bring their families to watch. Never could get that."

"Sounds pretty dumb." James tilted his head to the side, and Nate could see a smirk pulling at the corner of his mouth, "Got that out of your system before you got hitched?"

Nate stilled for a brief moment, trying to keep his voice level as he answered, "Yeah... it was a different life before we got married. I was a different person back then." As he spoke, he realized how true the words were—and how desperately he wanted them to stay true.

But James didn't seem to notice the hesitation. He nodded simply, "Yeah, gettin' hitched will do that to a man." He blew out a breath and stood, "Well, I'm gonna pop back across the street and see if my guest is hungry yet. If so, I may consider feeding him." Laughing at his own joke, James headed for the door.

But Nate sat there after the Sheriff left, staring at the deck of cards and wondering whether the change in him since marriage was to be a temporary change, or a permanent one.

***** ******

THIRTEEN

Saturday dawned with clear skies and a promise of sunshine. Nate had slept little the night before, despite having a separate room that didn't have people running in and out all night. He felt bad for Mary; she'd gotten no rest at all, but she wouldn't leave Clara's side for more than a few minutes at a time.

He had woken early, eaten breakfast, and was working on his third cup of coffee when he heard the door open. He looked up as James stepped in and stood by the door, focusing on him from across the room. "Can you use a hammer?"

Nate blinked twice before answering. "Yes, Sir..."

"Told you I'd have you some work while you're here—something to keep you busy—and well, it'll keep your mind off your little girl..."

Nate chuckled as he stood, dropping a two-bit piece on the table, "I'm ready to work... plus I'm fairly sure Miss Maude is tired of filling my coffee cup."

"Nah," James grinned as he held the door open, "But, I'm sure she'd rather be filling Earl's cup..." He nodded to an older man at a corner table. "But that's another story."

Nate grimaced at the thought of two old people sparkin' each other. It was as bad as thinking about his parents kissing.

Ick! He shook his head slowly. That was a memory he'd be happy to put out of his mind.

He followed James down to the livery at the edge of town where the holster had two saddled horses waiting for them. Nate grinned, looking forward to being in a saddle again after all the walking he'd done in the last week. He swung up easily and rode slowly after James through town and onto the trail.

Unfortunately, it was only a short ride out of town to the house, and Nate had barely settled in the saddle before it was time to dismount.

Nate swung down from the saddle and looked around. The house was a neat little cabin a short way from town, and it looked like there had been a good bit of work done on it recently.

James had already started pulling the saddle from his horse, "Thought everything was ready, but the roof got to leaking yesterday in the rain. Figured we'd get some new shakes on."

Nate grimaced as he looked at the roof. It was probably ten feet to the lower edge, with a sharp angle upward to the peak. It wasn't that he was scared of heights; he just didn't know if he wanted to be that high off the ground. "It's been a bit since I've done roof work... you want me to cut the shakes?"

"That's fine." He pointed to a pile of wood across from the corral, "Everything you need is over there."

Nate nodded, and quickly unsaddled his horse, turning it loose into the corral. When he first made his way west, he had worked for a while in Tennessee cutting shakes; it been a while since he'd done it, but it came back to him quickly.

They worked until late morning in effective silence; James stayed up on the roof while Nate cut a large stack of shakes. Once there were enough to cover the entire roof, they began hauling them up.

Around noon the older man from the restaurant, Earl, dropped by with a basket from Maude's. He said little, other than his need to get back to town and left quickly.

They took a brief lunch—James ate in a silent fervor, his mind focused somewhere else. It wasn't until Nate stood to get a drink that he focused on him.

"Oh, sorry. Did you need something?"

Nate held up the cup he had filled from the bucket, "I've got it."

James chuckled, "Sorry, I was used to working with Earl... He's old... and doesn't talk much."

Nate waved dismissively, "No problem. I'd have probably cut my toes off if I got to talking too much while I worked."

They shared a quiet laugh, and James offered, "Earl needed a break. He's watching the jail while I'm here."

"Well, that's probably for the best." Given the Sheriff's reaction when he found out Alfred was there, having someone else watch him was probably a good thing. He looked around, "This is a nice little spread. How long have you been here?"

"Never lived here. This was old Widow Johnson's house... she lived here a bunch of years. She passed not too long back and left it to Catherine."

"Oh," Nate nodded thoughtfully, "That was nice of her."

"Yeah... it's a nice spread, just needed some care. Widow Johnson's husband died a good time back. Ted, and a few other men in the area tried to help her when they could, but it needed more care than what they could spare. I've been getting it ready for me and Catherine."

"Looks like you've been doing a lot. Nice spot too— close to town."

"Yeah, and it was kindly unexpected." He chuckled, "I'd been wanting to propose, but couldn't rightly ask her to come live in the jail with me." He blanched at the memory, "Finally, I decided I was gonna build a cabin on some of my brother's land." He jerked his thumb to the south, "Raise some cattle. I was going to have to give up being Sheriff though...." He shook his head, "So I proposed, and that was when she told me this place was hers."

Nate grinned, "Well, that worked out well."

"Eh, so-so, anyway. Earl's still droning on and on about giving up ranching. Wanted to give me his spread so's he could retire and move into town." He leaned in, whispering comically, "Though it's likely he just wanted to spark Miss Maude."

Nate jerked his head erect, "Wait, Earl? The old..." He grimaced and restarted, "Er... well, the gentleman that dropped off lunch is your brother?" He looked at James skeptically, "He looks old enough to be your grandpa."

"Ha!" James blasted as he jumped up and did a quick dance, "That is hilarious!"

Nate watched as James, who was obviously tickled by the comment, celebrated the moment. "Are you alright?"

James wiped tears from his eyes as he sat back down, "Oh, that's good. I won't tell him it was you who said that, he might shoot you, but I have to tell him..." That set him off into another fit of laughter that lasted several minutes.

Nate sat, watching skeptically as James finally settled down. "Are you alright?"

"I've been having people tell us they thought he was my Pa for years. He argues—said they're just funnin' 'cause we look the same age."

"He thinks you look...?" Nate chuckled, "Well, I s'pose that's all depends on how good your eyesight is."

James evidently thought that was hilarious as well and struggled to finish his food through fits of laughter.

After they finished lunch, they climbed onto the roof and started placing the shingles. It was hot work on the roof, even with the cooler temperatures. Nate could feel a trail of sweat running down his back as they added the shingles, and by early afternoon they were finished.

"Whooee..." James wiped at his forehead with a rag, "I wasn't expecting it to be this hot."

"It is hot," Nate admitted. He was looking forward to climbing down and getting a drink.

James thumped his forehead, "Nate, I forgot to tell you, the Marshal was busy yesterday, but wants to talk to you about Alfred today."

Nate bit his lip, not especially thrilled with talking to another lawman, but he answered as cheery as he could, "No problem. When?"

James gave him a measured look, "That is the question, I s'pose. He's been spending most of his time with the Doc, but since she's been busy, he'll likely make time for you this evening."

Nate lifted an eyebrow but simply answered, "Right."

"I'm serious, you watch..." He was cut off as his hammer slid toward the edge of the roof and he dove for it, narrowly avoiding falling off the edge.

"Whoa there, Sheriff," Nate laughed as he reached to help him, "That hammer will survive a fall. You might not."

James gave him a sour look as he pulled himself up. "*Pfff*... Youngster thinks he has all the answers. I'll tell you..."

"Youngster?" Nate laughed, cutting him off. "What are you, thirty? I think I'll trust my answers, considering the answers you have just about took you off the edge of the roof!"

"I'm comin' up on thirty-four this year, as a matter of fact. And I'll have you know..." He trailed off for a moment, then took a more serious tone. "Hey, speaking of having all the answers, I know it's hard to sit and wait with yer little girl stove up, but I wanted to see if you'd like to come to Church tomorrow. You met the Parson already—he's a good man."

Nate grimaced, "Well, I dunno... me and God ain't exactly on good speaking terms."

James guffawed, shaking his head, "Only people I ever heard say they was on good speaking terms with God were fools that God probably wouldn't have a conversation with." He waved dismissively, "Nah, you come. You'll enjoy it."

Nate shrugged, "Alright, we'll see." He had no real intention of going and just wanted to end the subject peacefully.

But as they worked to put the tools away, the invitation to Church burned in Nate's mind.

***** ******

Once they finished putting up their tools, Nate and James rode back to town. James headed straight to the jail to check on his prisoner, while Nate went to the hotel to check on Mary and Clara before going to clean up. He wanted to get some of the sweat off him before time to meet the Marshal.

After taking a quick bath, Nate went back over to the restaurant and ordered a coffee while he waited. He was nervous about talking to the Marshal but was focused on keeping a calm demeanor. He knew the first thing that would give him away was a guilty look.

Nate was halfway through his second cup of coffee when a well-dressed young man came in and looked around the restaurant. He wasn't much older than he was, probably twenty-five or so, with dark hair and a low-slung pistol. Once he spotted Nate, he made a beeline for his table. Nate could see the badge on the man's shirt and knew it was the Marshal. As he approached the table the man smiled broadly, "Are you Nate?"

Nate stood quickly, offering his hand, "Yes, Sir." He waved to the chair across from him, "Have a seat."

"Thanks." The Marshal offered briefly as he sat down, "Well, Nate; I'm Marshal Lucas Sterling. I just need to ask you a few questions about the other day." He smoothed out a small notebook on the table, "Your name is...?"

"Nathaniel Taylor."

The Marshal wrote that down, "And on Thursday October 17th, you were riding on a stage heading to Cobbinsville?"

"Yes, Sir... well through Cobbinsville. We—myself, my wife, and daughter—were heading to Dana for the train." Nate wanted to be certain he plugged that information into the Marshal's mind before the man thought about any wanted posters he may have seen."

The Marshal noted that, "Alright, and it was boarded by a man named Alfred, correct?" Nate nodded simply, and the Marshal leaned back, "Tell me what you saw."

"Well, Sir, we were already on board the stage when Alfred boarded near the Colorado border... I can't remember the name of the town though." Nate took several minutes and detailed Alfred's behavior on the stage and continued the story through to Cobbinsville.

The Marshal nodded, "So, Alfred got off the stage and entered the store?"

"Yes," Nate nodded, "I was heading in to buy Clara some nickel candy, and he was arguing with a woman—who I later learned was named Catherine—

Steve C. Roberts

then he grabbed her arm and started yanking her around."

"And then...?"

Nate smiled grimly, "Well, Sir... I stopped him."

"Good." The Marshal finished writing in the notebook and closed it with a smile. "That was all I needed from you, and..." He pulled out a watch and looked at the time, "I need to meet someone else in a little bit." He grinned and stood to his feet, shoving the notebook in his pocket. "Alfred was already wanted on multiple other charges, including murder, so I do not believe they will be taking time to press any other charges... I wanted your statement in case they choose to bring those as well."

Nate scratched under his eye with his thumb, "Alright, just let me know if you need anything else."

"I will. And thank you, Nate." He started to leave, but paused for a moment, "Maggie mentioned that your little girl was very ill. I wanted you to know that we're praying for her." He smiled broadly, "She lucked out with Maggie, she's the best Doctor I know."

Nate felt a smile tug at the corner of his mouth at the Marshal's blatant familiarity with the Doc—he assumed she was the one the Marshal was sparkin'. "Well, she's been taking excellent care of Clara, and we really appreciate the prayers."

The Marshal gave a curt nod and headed for the stairs; apparently, he was also staying in the building. Nate grinned as he stood, the bright side of the situation was that the good Marshal seemed to be thoroughly enamored with the Doc... and that lack of focus was probably a good thing for him and Mary.

***** ******

It wasn't until Doc Maggie was getting ready to leave to meet her beau that Mary found out he was the United States Deputy Marshal that was in town to take Alfred back east. When Doc Maggie had told her, she'd felt a cold knot of fear in the pit of her stomach, hoping he didn't recognize Nate from any reward posters. Of course, his was recent enough that it may not have circulated, but hers...

Hers was a different story. Her poster had surely been in circulation for months, and since there probably weren't too many women's faces adorning those posters, a U.S. Marshal would probably recognize her easily.

However, she wasn't planning on giving the good Marshal that opportunity. She had no intention in leaving the room and giving him an opportunity to see her, and she was fairly certain that he wouldn't come up to see a sick child. Doc Maggie had told her he was leaving on the stage Monday, and that would be that.

She had been on pins and needles waiting for what seemed like a fortnight, but at the sound of boots on the stairs she froze, staring at the door. They passed by, heading to a room further down the hall, and she waited. Another minute passed and another set of boots; she recognized the step as Nate's and tensed as he opened the door and stepped in. As soon as Nate stepped in the room and closed the door she frantically whispered, "How did it go?"

Nate twisted his mouth in a smile and shrugged, "Pretty straightforward I s'pose. He just asked about everything I saw with Alfred from the time he got on the stage, until... well, when I punched him."

"Did the Marshal act like..." She tightened her mouth in a thin line, "You know... like you looked familiar?"

Nate laughed, a loud burst of noise that made her jump. Grinning, he took a seat in the empty chair and quietly added, "You know, he could've been holding a wanted poster with my face on it in his hand, and he probably wouldn't have thought twice." He jerked his thumb at the door, "He was more worried about meeting someone for dinner."

"Doc Maggie?"

"The same." He shook his head, obviously amused.

Mary twisted her mouth disapprovingly, "She was pretty excited about meeting him, I think, and that's not necessarily a good thing. Not until after we can leave."

Nate nodded slowly, "Nah, I wouldn't worry. It's probably good for us that they are so focused on each other... well, and Alfred."

Despite her reservation, Mary felt a smile pull at her mouth. It *had* been sweet to watch Doc Maggie fret and primp when she was going to see the Marshal. She could tell the woman had strong feelings for the man. Her eyes cut toward Nate, kind of like she...

She shook off the thought and glanced over at Clara. She was sleeping fitfully—her temperature was lower, but she wasn't out of danger yet. "I'll feel better once we can leave."

"It'll be fine." Nate offered quietly, "You'll see."

Mary nodded; her lips tight. She just hoped he was right.

***** ******

Steve C. Roberts

FOURTEEN

Nate felt strange walking into a Church... he hadn't been in one since his Ma died and that was back in '65, before his Pa had made it home from the war.

He'd initially planned to stay back at the hotel. Even this morning when he woke up, he hadn't planned on going, but everyone else was heading that way except Mary, Clara, and the Doc. Plus, since James had personally invited him to Church, he couldn't figure out a nice way to say no.

Of course, with Clara sick, and the female Doc hovering around... it just felt uncomfortable to be there anyway.

Though not quite as uncomfortable as this.

He nodded a greeting to Mrs. Maude and James' brother Earl—struggling as he took a seat in the back to keep the images of old people romance out of his mind.

"What are ya sitting back here for?"

The sudden question made him jump, and he turned quickly. James was at the end of the pew, watching him skeptically. He half stood, embarrassed. "Is this someone's seat?"

James grinned, "Well, no... but I invited you to Church. You're supposed to sit with me."

"Oh. I'm sorry." He nervously followed James forward to the front row where a young woman was waiting on the pew. As if being in Church wasn't uncomfortable enough on its own, now James wanted him to sit on the front pew? He nodded a greeting to the young woman, recognizing her from the store and smiled hesitantly, "Ma'am... nice to see you."

"Nice to see you as well." She offered with a sad smile. "We heard your daughter was sick. We've been praying for her."

"Thank you." He really was appreciative of that. He figured that Clara needed God's attention, and since he wasn't on good terms with the Lord, the more Church people praying for her, the better.

He sat on the other end of the pew, leaving enough room for James and probably four or five other people.

A few minutes later a woman came in carrying a large case, and Catherine stood and followed her to the front, talking a seat at the piano while the woman sat down the case and pulled out a cello.

His Ma had always loved music. Back home, their neighbor had been a music teacher, and the sounds of cello and violin were always in the air.

It was one of the few things he missed about home.

Catherine began playing first, then the woman with the cello joined in. It was a beautiful melody that others in the room took as a signal to find their seats.

They sung through several hymns before the Parson got up to speak. Nate felt awkward sitting on the front row. It was like the Parson had direct aim at him... kind of like that Preacher back home had been like when he was a boy. Staring straight at him and yelling about evil.

But this Parson surprised him in that. He didn't yell at all, which was a good start in Nate's mind. He just started talking about a man named Jacob.

It didn't take long before Nate was engrossed in the story. Jacob was the son of Isaac and Rebekah. He had gone down a rough path in life, but when he got right, God changed his name to Israel—new behavior, new person, new name. Those were things he remembered from when his Ma read him stories from the Bible when he was a boy.

He knew Jacob had been rough, but he didn't recall his Ma telling him just *how* horrible Jacob had been before God renamed him. He was a flat-out thief, stole from his brother, lied to his father, worked hard to rip off his uncle... and those were just the things recorded in the Bible. Goodness knows what else the man did.

But then a great thing happened. He wrestled with God and—more specifically—came to the point where he admitted what he was.

And God forgave him.

Nate was mulling that over when the Parson had them turn to the New Testament. He flipped the pages in the borrowed Bible and listened as the Parson continued.

"In the Gospel of John, we see Jesus talking to a woman who'd been caught in adultery... some people say she was a woman of ill repute. But, watch this... *'When Jesus had lifted up himself, and saw none but the woman, he said unto her, Woman, where are those thine accusers? hath no man condemned thee? She said, No man, Lord. And Jesus said unto her, Neither do I condemn thee: go, and sin no more.'"* The Parson looked over the audience, "That's what Christ is interested in, not you being some perfect person who'd never made a mistake, but living up to it, and committing to not do it again." He nodded curtly and closed his Bible, "So, the choice is yours, what will you do? Let's pray."

As Nate bowed his head, the thought occurred to him that not only was this what he needed to hear, but that God had cared enough about him to have the Parson prepare this message. Matter of fact, everything he had been through had brought him to this point— and now he had the choice. Was he going to continue to lie, cheat, and steal? Or was he going to go and sin no more?

***** ******

Mary leaned back in her chair and closed her eyes. She was tired of being in the little room. Clara was starting to improve, but still slept most of the time. She had hardly seen Nate—he'd spent all day Saturday with the Sheriff, and since Miss Maude had given him another room to sleep in, they hadn't spoken much beyond him poking his head in to check on them. Doc Maggie had been in and out all through the night. She had come in early that morning to stay with her while Nate went to Church with the Sheriff.

If she were honest, she would have to admit that she was concerned by the amount of time Nate had spent with the Sheriff... he had worked with him the day before and seemed to have struck up a cordial relationship with the man.

Of course, the Sheriff probably felt like he owed Nate for punching Alfred... and the closer Nate was to the Sheriff, the less likely it would be for the Sheriff to turn him in, if it *did* come to that.

So, she supposed it was a good thing. Better a Church than a bar, that was certain... but she did miss him being there with her constantly.

She glanced over at Doc Maggie; she was staring out the window, seemingly lost in thought. She seemed like a really nice woman and had been constantly reassuring her that Clara would be all right. "So, you said you were going to take part in the Sheriff's wedding?"

Doc Maggie had turned when she spoke, but her face lit up at the question, "Oh, yes. I can't wait. Partly because my..." she smiled, "Well, Lucas will be here for the wedding."

"Ah," Mary grinned, "And Lucas is your beau?"

Blushing profusely, Doc shrugged, "Well, he hasn't exactly asked, but he's..." She leaned over and whispered conspiratorially, "He's riding out this evening to talk with my father."

"Oh, really?" The excitement Doc felt was palpable, "I'm glad for you."

"Thank you. He's very special."

Mary blanched as memories from the past flooded her—how Horace had acted when he first started coming around, "Well, just bear in mind, all men act special... right up until they have you. Then the real them comes out."

There was a long pause, and Doc Maggie asked softly, "Mary...is Nate hurting you?"

Mary jerked her head up, "Nate, oh, goodness no. He's always been nothing but kind."

Doc Maggie pursed her lips, obviously unconvinced, "That didn't sound like 'nothing but kind.'"

Mary bit her lip in consternation. She shouldn't have let her guard down and said something. That was really going to make some waves if the Doc said anything to anyone. "I was involved with another man, before Nate... He wasn't like Nate." She looked down at her lap, hoping that was enough information to keep the Doc from prying further.

"I see." There was a quiet pause before she added, "But you are alright now, then?"

"As alright as I can be." She looked up, "But, enough about the past... Yesterday you mentioned that your Lucas is a United States Deputy Marshal...?"

Doc Maggie smiled knowingly, obviously understanding Mary wanted to change the subject. "Yes, he is."

Mary raised an eyebrow with a smile, "Well... tell me. How did you meet him?"

Doc Maggie leaned back in her chair, smiling at a memory, "His horse drug him into town unconscious with a snakebite... he almost died."

Mary nodded slowly. She didn't know if that were a joke or real, "That's... romantic."

Doc Maggie waved a hand dismissively, "Oh, silly, it was more than that. While he was recuperating, we talked and talked... he's..." She blushed, "Not like other men that I've dealt with."

It was Mary's turn to raise an eyebrow. Just Doc Maggie's tone spoke volumes about her previous dealings. But, instead of pursuing that line, she nodded simply. "What makes him so different?"

Still smiling, Doc Maggie waved a hand, "It's so many things, but it started with absolute acceptance of me, including the fact that I'm a doctor." She thought for a moment, "Especially the fact that I'm a doctor." She closed her eyes as if trying to see a memory, "When he first heard I was a doctor, he didn't make a big deal of it." She nodded to herself, "I had just told him that I was the one treating him, and instead of complaining, he said something I'll never forget. *'Most men act before they think, most ladies think before they act. If I'd had a man Doctor, he'd have probably cut off my leg...'*" She trailed off, looking at Mary expectantly.

Mary nodded slowly—it was the only reaction she could think of. She personally didn't see much romance in him saying that, but she wasn't a Doctor—or snake-bit—so maybe it meant more to them because of the situation. "That's awful sweet..." She offered hesitantly.

Doc Maggie tilted her head, "Well, not exactly sweet, but definitely not closed minded like a lot of men." She scoffed, "I've met so many men that think only of themselves, and how everything will affect them. Lucas seems to really care about others... he puts others first, without thought for himself."

"That sounds like Nate..." She blurted without thinking, "I mean...," she gestured to Clara, "He doesn't hesitate to put himself out just for our comfort." She smiled, gesturing to the doll that the little girl was still clutching in her sleep, "She'd lost her favorite doll when the wagon..." She trailed off; painfully aware she had almost said too much. Shaking

214

her head, she continued, "He spent the next few days whittling that for her. When we got to a town, he offered to buy her a nice, new doll—she refused, and hasn't let go of that one."

"That's awful sweet." Doc Maggie smiled warmly, "You're very lucky to have him."

Mary's brow furrowed as she considered that statement. She was lucky to have Nate... but how long was that going to last? To the train? To California? Was she going to keep him, and if so, what was it going to take?

***** ******

After the service Nate stood quietly near the front of the Church waiting on the Parson. He was leaning against the banister with his hands jammed in his pockets, because he could feel them shaking every time he pulled them out.

Part of him wanted to get this right, and of course, the other part of him wanted to light a shuck and get out of there. But, about the time he decided to follow that idea, the Parson turned, "Nate... you look like you'd like to talk."

"Yes, Sir... Parson. If you have a moment." They walked off to the side, "I just had a question about your message." His throat suddenly felt dry. He swallowed with difficulty, then pressed on. "When Jacob wrestled with God, he admitted to God what he was, and what

215

he'd done... but what about the people he'd lied to and took from... did he go admit it to them too?"

There was a hint of a smile at the corner of the Parson's mouth when he answered, "Well, I'll be honest with you, Nate... that is a direction that God will give the individual he is dealing with. I don't believe there is always a "this must happen" answer to that question."

Nate lifted an eyebrow, confused. "What do you mean?"

The Parson chuckled, "Just what I said." He gestured to the departing congregation, "I could tell everyone in this room what I think they should do, but they would be doing just that—what I think they should do. But, I'm not God." He blew out a short breath, "Nate, God gave us the Bible to know His principles and His standards... and there are some things that are clear-cut in that. But, in this case..." He shook his head, "You'll have to let God guide you. Pray. See what He shows you."

"Well, Parson..." Nate started hesitantly, "Me and God ain't exactly on speaking terms."

"Let me ask you, Nate—was there a time in your life when you accepted Christ's free pardon?"

"Yes, Sir... I was a boy." He remembered the service—it had actually been the last one his Pa had went to. He'd just turned six the week before, and his Ma had sewed him his first pair of long pants and bought him a pair of shoes. There'd been this woman who'd taken the Bible and showed him about the gift Christ offered, and he'd been excited to kneel and pray.

His Pa, however, was offended that Nate had scuffed his new shoes 'kneeling on the floor like some animal,' and refused to ever go back—or let Nate. Of course, his Ma took him after Pa left for the war, but it never felt right. By the time his Ma passed, he hadn't been inside a Church for a long time. "But, a lot of things have changed between then and now."

The Parson grinned, "Let me tell you a story. There was a farmer who used to go on long drives with his wife, and she would sit snuggled next to him in the carriage. Well, as they got older the Farmer's wife got to setting a little further and further away until she was at the other side of the carriage."

Nate lifted an eyebrow, wondering if the Parson had forgotten why he was there... Did he think he was there for marital advice?

"Well..." The Parson continued, "One day out on the road, they passed a newlywed couple all snuggled up for a ride. Well, the old farmer's wife looked at them and said, 'Look at that. Remember when we used to ride that close?'" The Parson paused for a moment, "Well, the old farmer looked at his wife and said, 'Well, I ain't moved.'"

Nate nodded slowly, hoping the confusion he felt wasn't written all over his face.

Unfortunately, it must have been, because the Parson chuckled softly, "Nate think about it. You're just like the farmer's wife. Once you established that relationship with God, you are His. He loves you—but when you sin, you scoot further and further away from God. The thing about it is, He's still there, waiting for you to just scoot closer to Him. He hasn't moved, Nate. He wants you to. If you want to find God, hit your knees and start looking."

Nate looked down at the floor as what the Parson was saying finally made sense. God was still interested in him... but he was going to have to move God's direction. "Thank you, Parson."

The Parson clasped his shoulder, "I'm here if you need me, but I really think what you need more is to spend some time seeking God."

"Yes, Sir." Nate shook the man's hand, then headed toward the door. He figured that trying to talk to God was something he probably shouldn't put off any longer.

As he stepped out on the porch, the Sheriff and his fiancé were outside waiting. "Nate, thanks for coming today. I was talking with Catherine, and we wanted to have dinner with you and your wife this evening. Nothing fancy, just down in the restaurant, close to your little girl."

Nate wasn't certain if Mary would be interested; the more he talked to the Sheriff, the more nervous she got. "I'll have to check with her. She might not want Clara to be alone."

James laughed, "I understand that. Well, we can plan on it, and if it doesn't work out just send word."

Nate agreed, and they parted company. As Nate headed for the hotel, he found himself looking forward to taking some time to pray.

***** ******

FIFTEEN

Doc Maggie was thrilled when Mary asked her to watch Clara while she and Nate went downstairs for a quick meal. As Mary stepped out of the room, she realized it was the first time she had been out of the room for more than a few minutes since Clara got sick.

She watched Nate carefully as they sat at the table waiting. He had been acting different that afternoon. Ever since he came back from Church, he had been quiet... well, quieter than usual. He sat staring, brow furrowed, at the coffee in his cup for several minutes before she finally said something. "Are you alright?"

He looked up, startled. "Yes, sorry." He shook his head, "Just had a lot on my mind since Church today."

Mary grimaced, "I never did ask, how was it?"

He met her eyes, "The Parson was really..." he twisted his mouth in a half-smile, "...well, unexpected."

She leaned forward, interested. "What did you expect?"

"I dunno. I mean, I spoke with him that first day, and he seemed down to earth... but, he just has a way of telling you what you need to hear, the way you need to hear it."

"Oh." She had only spoken with the Parson twice; when he'd come over to let her know they couldn't leave town, and when he and his wife came up earlier to pray over Clara. He seemed nice enough—though she had spent more time talking to his wife, Anna. "I don't know. The last preacher I heard kept yelling about how everyone was going to burn." She shook her head, "Seems to me that might be true for a lot of people, but they might respond better to talking about how God loves them and doesn't want them to burn."

"Hmmm, I can see that." He shrugged noncommittally, "Well, Parson William didn't say anything about people burning—he was talking 'bout people who get sideways with God, how they can get back to where they should be."

She wrinkled her nose slightly, "And how was that?"

"Well..." His brow furrowed as he thought, "It's like riding together in a wagon with God, and you scoot over to the side. You just need to scoot back... but, in prayer."

Mary blinked a few times before responding. "That sounded convoluted, but alright..."

Nate's brow furrowed, and he tried again, "Well, Parson told it better, but... wait, here's the Sheriff and his intended..."

Mary looked up from the table and her smile faded as she instantly recognized the Sheriff's soon to be bride as they approached. Of all the people in the world that could have possibly shown up to dinner, it had to be Catherine Woodfield.

Suddenly everything clicked into place, and Mary cursed her own stupidity. Alfred coming here to see a woman. Of course, it had to be Catherine. She had just never pictured prim and proper Catherine Woodfield living in a dusty town two-thousand miles from Philadelphia.

He family home was directly next to the Woodfield's, and even though she was several years younger than Catherine, they had socialized on multiple occasions.

Way too many to expect Catherine not to recognize her.

As Nate and James exchanged pleasantries, Mary stared down at the table, refusing to meet Catherine's eyes. She *had* recognized her... hadn't she? Wasn't it her? Could it be she was mistaken? That it was simply another woman named Catherine that looked like her? A doppelgänger of looks and name? Mary slowly looked up and met Catherine's gaze... she could see the recognition on her face. Nope, definitely her.

She looked back down quickly. So much for Catherine not recognizing her. But, how could she not? She had sat across from Catherine dozens of times over the years... even listening to her blather on about her fiancé Alfred, and what her plans were after they wed.

She mentally berated herself. Alfred. Throughout all of this it had never occurred to her that *she* was the reason Alfred was here. She should have guessed, but it never...

And now she was here, about to marry a town Sheriff?

She glanced at Nate as she suppressed the urge to jump up and run. Did Nate know? Is that why he brought her to dinner, so the Sheriff could arrest her? No, he wouldn't do that... especially not with his own neck on the line.

"So, Mary..." Catherine started in a mild tone.

Mary felt the question behind the innocent opening, and looked up, composing herself and smiling demurely, "Yes?"

"We've been praying for Clara..." Catherine enunciated the name clearly, and looked over at James, "The whole Church has... I am so sorry I hadn't made it up to see you before now."

Mary's lips tightened for a moment, "Oh, I understand..." She looked down at the table, "I'm sorry... I just..."

"Are you alright?" Nate asked, suddenly sounding concerned.

"I just feel faint..." She fanned herself vigorously, "I need to lie down." She looked at Nate, "I am so sorry, can you take me to the room."

Nate moved so quickly his chair hit the wall with a thud, "Let me help you."

Part of her felt bad at the note of terror in his voice. James had also stood, and was shifting from foot to foot, obviously at a loss. She glanced at Catherine as she stood, surprised at the look of fear and sadness—she didn't know what she should have expected, but it wasn't that.

Nate held her arm and led her up the stairs to the room, but she kept going past to the extra room Maude had given Nate. She needed to talk to him without the Doc listening.

***** ******

James stood nervously watching the couple climb the steps, but as soon as Mary and Nate disappeared at the top, Catherine turned to him, "James, I need you to do me a favor. Don't ask questions, but never give Alfred an opportunity to see Mary."

James lifted an eyebrow. "Well, that would be kind of difficult—and too late—since they rode in on the stage together... but I am curious as to why."

She glanced nervously at the steps, "It's a long story..."

James picked up his coffee cup, "Then give me the brief version."

She grunted, obviously frustrated, "Fine... Her and her little sister lived next door, her parents died in an accident, and the next thing we knew she was married to this horrible man—Horace Cooper—who incidentally was a friend of Alfred's. There was a constable involved... rumors were that he'd been paid off, but the details were sketchy." She took a quick breath and looked at the stairs, "Anyway, people started to notice things about them... Horace was drinking up all her parent's money and passerby's heard yelling and things breaking almost every evening... some people reported seeing bruises on her on the rare occasion he let her out... They knew Horace was abusing her, maybe even them both. But nobody *did* anything." She looked down. "One night we came home, and the house was all lit up. Police everywhere. Horace was dead—he had been shot—and her and her sister were gone. Disappeared. At first, they thought it may have been a murder/kidnapping, but the investigation showed that she'd shot him and left."

James set his cup down on the table, a scowl on his face as he mulled her story over. "So, Nate's wife killed her... husband? But it wasn't murder?"

Catherine blew out a long breath. When he said it like that it sounded so convoluted that it made her eyes want to cross. "No, everyone in town knew he was abusing her... and possibly her little sister. As I said, when they investigated the scene it was obvious that he had been drunk and tearing up the house, so the Judge refused to press charges... the only reason they've been looking for her was concern for her and her sister's wellbeing."

James sat back in his chair, "Well, why didn't you say something to her?"

Catherine felt her face heat up, "I didn't know what her current state was... I mean, does she know that she's not wanted? She was scared when she recognized me, so I didn't think so, unless it is because her new husband doesn't know..." She trailed off and looked down at her lap. "So, is she hiding her past from just him, or everyone?"

James nodded, "Well, alright... the question is, what will she do now?"

Catherine jerked her head up sharply, "What do you mean?"

"Since she recognized you, will she run?"

"I don't know..."

James leaned back in his chair and took a sip of his coffee. "Then I s'pose you ought to go find out."

***** ******

As soon as they stepped into the room, Mary spun to face Nate, "We need to leave now!"

Nate recoiled, suddenly wary, "What's wrong?"

Mary looked over back at the door, worried they may have been followed. "Catherine. She knows."

Nate's eyes widened, "What? How?"

Mary paced quickly back and forth, "I knew her... she lived next door to us... back home."

Lips tight, Nate stepped over to the bed, "Should I pack?"

Mary buried her face in her hands. She didn't know what to do. "We can't leave without Clara!" She looked up, tears already forming at the corner of her eyes, "We can't move her..."

A light knock sounded at the door, and Mary froze, midsentence. She looked to Nate, who had already palmed his pistol and stepped between her and the door.

"Should I open it?"

Catherine's voice was muffled as it came through the door. "Rosemary... it's me. Catherine. I just want to talk."

Nate turned his head to face her and lifted an eyebrow.

Mary chewed her lip and nodded. It was too late to just run. Maybe she could talk Catherine into taking care of Clara.

Nate slid his pistol into the holster and pulled the door open. Catherine was alone in the hall, her hands clasped in front of her dress.

"May I speak with Rosemary...? Alone?"

Nate glanced over his shoulder and met Mary's eyes. She swallowed hard and nodded, "Go ahead."

Nate stepped aside and allowed Catherine into the room, and with one last glance to Mary, stepped out into the hall and pulled the door shut behind him.

As soon as the door clicked shut, Catherine turned to Mary, "I am so glad you're safe... Everyone has been so worried about you."

Mary stared, wide eyed, not quite knowing what to do. Her eyes cut to the door, wondering if the good Sheriff was standing outside ready to arrest her. Was Nate with him? She didn't know... She felt hot tears at the corner of her eyes as she thought of Clara all alone. "Can you..." Her voice cracked, "Can you wait at least until Clara is better?"

Catherine blinked several times before answering, "Wait? Wait for what?"

"For your Sheriff to arrest me."

Catherine stepped back as if she's been slapped, "What? What for?" Comprehension suddenly dawned on her face, "You mean for Horace?" She shook her head, "Oh, Rosemary, nobody wants to arrest you. Everyone knew that Horace was..." She looked down "...horrible... you did nothing wrong."

Mary's legs felt weak, and she staggered against the bureau, "What?" She was certain she hadn't heard her correctly.

Catherine moved across the room and embraced Rosemary tightly, "Since you disappeared, everyone has been worried about you. They've been looking for you and Sarah to make certain you were all right." Her voice broke, "I'm so sorry... the only reason I didn't say anything downstairs was because I didn't know what Nate knew, and didn't want to be the one to blurt it out."

Mary felt sick at her stomach. The faintness she had feigned downstairs suddenly manifested itself. "Nate knows... he..." She looked up at Catherine. "Horace was beating her. I had to stop him."

Catherine squeezed her tighter, and Mary sobbed. All the fear, all the worry. Everything they had gone through in the last several months had been for nothing.

"You don't have to run anymore." Catherine murmured, "You're safe... you can go home if you want, or you can stay here."

Mary stepped back suddenly, wiping at her face. "But, what about Nate?"

***** ******

Nate walked slowly down the steps, his mind racing as the Sheriff came into view. He felt a brief surge of anger at James—the Sheriff was sitting at the table, calmly sipping his coffee while Nate's life was falling apart upstairs.

He tamped the feeling down quickly; it wasn't James' fault, and he knew it. He reached the bottom of the steps and faced the Sheriff.

"Well, have a seat there, Pard..." James gestured to the seat across from him.

Nate crossed to the table and sat down, watching James closely. He wasn't acting remotely threatening—he simply looked curious.

"So..." James trailed off expectantly, apparently waiting for him to fill in the blanks.

"Well, let's start with what Miss Catherine told you." Nate countered quietly.

James quirked an eyebrow, "Your wife had some previous issues. Not mine to spill if'n you don't know the details."

Nate tilted his head, his curiosity piqued, "I know about her past..."

"No, you don't." James shook his head, "Well, I don't think you know it all, anyway." He gestured to the stairs, James picked up and took a slow sip of his coffee, "Little girl acts like someone on the run... she's not."

Nate recoiled in surprise, "She's not?" His eyes narrowed, "Are you sure we're talking about the same thing? Her first husband?" Nate stopped talking, suddenly nervous he had said too much.

"Yup, and I meant what I said. Catherine told me all about her... well, first husband. It was considered self-defense. The law was never gonna press charges. They've been hunting her and the little girl just to be certain they're safe."

"Well..." Nate trailed off. He was surprised, well and obviously happy for her, but there was a myriad of other emotions running through him as well. He wasn't really sure how to respond. "I guess that's good."

"Good for her," James offered wryly, "It don't cure your ills though."

Nate stilled, unsure what the Sheriff was saying. "What?"

James shook his head sadly, "Boy, you're running from something in your past... I smelled it on you when I first met you." He fell quiet for a few moments, then continued. "What you need is to get over your past... it's like back when you were in diapers, and your Ma wanted you to use the outhouse. There were times you didn't make it. Times you failed and doodled in your diaper."

Nate lifted an eyebrow and stared in disbelief. After spending time with him he knew James was strange, but this had to be the strangest conversation he'd ever had, even with him.

Grinning, James continued, "Did you just live in your failure? Sit in that dirty diaper and relive your failure over and over again? Or did you clean up, and press on with life—and work to never doodle in your diaper again?"

Nate nodded slowly, "Well, I s'pose I cleaned up and pressed on."

"So, that's what you do now."

Nate smiled grimly, "Well, that sounds all good and fine... actually, I spent the afternoon prayin' about it. I want to get it right. I want to move forward... 'cept when I clean this up, it's not about just washing up... I might get hung." He tugged at his collar, as if he could feel the noose already.

James pursed his lips, "That does pose a problem, doesn't it?" He blew out a sharp breath, "So, come clean... what'cha do?"

Nate swallowed hard and nodded slowly, "Ok, well..." He decided to just come completely clean, "When I came west, I hooked up with these other guys..." He went on to explain how they started riding together, their plan to rob the bank, and how the rest got killed in the process. He ended with his escape and how he had found Mary and Clara at the wagon train.

James nodded thoughtfully, "Ok, three questions... first, did any of the townspeople get hurt?"

"No, sir... not that I'm aware of anyway." Nate thought for a moment, "I don't think any of us got off a shot." He looked down, "I dropped my gun on accident and never picked it back up." Thinking for a moment, he added. "Now, they did run into that band of Ute's when they were chasing me... but I don't know how that went."

James frowned, "Ok, well, I'm not going to worry about that right now." He thought for a moment, "Now, you said you left the gold there at the wagon train?"

Nate nodded, "Yes, sir. It felt cursed, I guess..."

"It was." He nodded curtly, "Ok, last question... where was this bank at anyway?"

"Little town in Colorado... Klein."

James' mouth twitched, "Klein. Northwestish part of the state?"

Nate's eyes narrowed, "Yes, Sir." The sound of a door opening upstairs caught his attention, and he looked up—Miss Catherine had started slowly down the steps, her face tight with emotion. He turned back to face James.

James watched her for a moment, his lips tight, "I rode through that part of country a few times." He stood slowly, "I'll tell you what, bank robbin' is serious business—you've seen that firsthand—but give me a few days to check things out."

"Alright..." Nate didn't really know what good that would do, except prolong the necktie party, but that was that.

James leaned in and tapped the table with his finger. "Now, let me tell you one thing. I don't want you making any decisions right now. You just wait, and I'll let you know. You're fine here, and that little girl still needs rest." He met his eyes, "You understand?"

Nate nodded slowly, "Yes, Sir."

"Alright then," James grinned, "Now go see your wife."

***** ******

234

Nate walked slowly up the stairs to the room. His mind was racing. He knew this was going to be life changing for them—this completely changed the foundation of their relationship—he just wondered how Mary was taking all of this.

He huffed out a quiet laugh. He didn't even know how *he* was taking it yet. He was mostly just confused. He'd spent all that time in prayer looking for answers for himself, and now it seemed like those answers were even further from him than when he began.

The fact was he cared for her, and when they were both wanted by the law, he had a hope of a future with her—they were already married, and so maybe one day she would come to feel for him like he felt for her.

Maybe eventually they could be a normal man and wife.

But now she was safe. She wasn't wanted. She had a life and a future—and even an inheritance—and he was a direct threat to all of that because as long as she was with him, she was aiding and abetting a criminal... which was a hanging offence.

He stepped into the room and closed the door behind him. Mary didn't turn; she was standing by the window, looking out. He stood quietly for a moment— he didn't even know what to say to her. "Mary?" He offered hesitantly as he took a step deeper into the room.

Mary spun from the window, and without a word launched herself across the room at him, wrapping him in a tight hug. "Did you hear?" She asked breathlessly, "Did the Sheriff tell you?"

Nate tensed when she grabbed him—it was the first time he'd been hugged by a woman since his Ma passed and old widow Winslow wrapped him in a bear hug at the funeral—and luckily, in her excitement, Mary hadn't noticed. He reminded himself that she *was* technically his wife and patted her back awkwardly, "Yeah, he said you were safe."

"We're safe. No charges." She stepped back and he could see the relief written on her face, "All this time, everything that has happened..." She shook her head, "I've been so worried."

"I'm happy for you—both of you, really." He smiled broadly... but it was a strange feeling; like the day after his Ma's funeral, when a friend of his was bragging that he'd got a new watch for his birthday. Trying to be happy for someone when your life was still in shambles. It was kind of like that.

But he wasn't going to ruin her moment with his woes.

Her face shone with excitement and she started talking rapid-fire. "Now... Well, I don't know what to do. Should I... no, it doesn't matter. We have to stay here until Clara is better anyway." She flitted around the room, back and forth. "Clara is starting to get better, but it will still be a few days before she could travel. We could go back to Philadelphia—the house is just waiting, and my father's business is still there—so money is no problem." She continued on for several minutes going back and forth with possibilities.

Nate leaned against the wall and watched her. She was flushed with excitement and it seemed like she'd already forgotten that they hadn't eaten dinner yet—not that he could stomach food at the moment. She kept going for a full ten minutes before she finally ran out of energy and sat on the edge of the bed.

She looked up at him, and her eyes narrowed. She opened her mouth to add something but, closed it sharply and stared at him. "What's wrong?" She demanded suddenly.

Nate shrugged, "Nothing."

She stared at him for several seconds, "No, something..." Her eyes widened with realization, "Oh... I'm so... I didn't think about your..."

Nate waved dismissively, "No, it isn't...I'm responsible for all my own choices."

"Still." She frowned and sat heavily on a chair. "I can't let anything happen to you. You can come back east with me. Nobody back east knows, and nobody has to."

He felt a brief surge of hope flood through him. It sounded good—well, anything that didn't involve a noose sounded good—but, staying with Mary and moving on together... He shook his head slowly. The fact was, he had already talked to James about it. He was going to face his past—whatever the cost—but he had no plans on telling her that right then. "What if they found out?"

"They won't." She insisted.

"They might." Nate blew out a long breath, "And then it could be bad for you." He was hoping she would see logic but could tell by the set of her jaw that—to her—the discussion was over.

"No, we'll be fine." Mary shook her head, "You'll see."

Nate bit his lip in frustration, but let the topic drop in the hopes that she would come to her senses by the time the Sheriff got back with him. He just hoped that James could arrange for prison time, or something other than hanging.

***** ******

SIXTEEN

James had been working hard to not smile as he and the Marshal waited for the stage to come in. Lucas had spent half the morning craning his neck as he kept an eye out for Doc Maggie. When she finally left the hotel and came over, Lucas settled down with a wide smile. Now that she had left, he was back to looking sour and craning his neck on the off chance that she came back.

He wondered absently if that was how he looked waiting for Catherine.

It was midmorning before they heard the stage rattling over the trail, but even though it was still a good way out the Marshal stood, "Alright, I guess I'll take custody of Mr. Beachem now."

James grinned and walked back to the cell, unlocking it with a large key. "Alright, Alfred. You are hereby transferred to the custody of the US Marshal service. Good luck."

The look Alfred gave him was anything but thankful, but he quietly stood and waited as they placed arm and leg irons on him for the transport.

Once he was secure, they marched him out the door onto the porch just as the stage pulled up in a whirl of dust. The driver was hollering instructions to the passengers as they started piling out and heading for the restaurant.

James grinned and stepped forward as one passenger stepped down, "Well, I'll be... Jesse. You made it early."

Jesse turned with a wide grin, "Yeah, I did," He offered slowly, then turned back to help a woman down. "Wouldn't miss meeting the little lady that was blind enough to accept your proposal." He turned back with a wry smile, "I had planned on having Madge try to talk some sense into her."

"Oh, no you don't, Jesse." The woman scolded, "Someone's got to corral James, and it's about time someone's offered." She looked at James, "Did she really shoot you? Or was that just Jesse funnin' me?"

James laughed, "No, Ma'am... she surely did." He clapped Jesse on the shoulder, "Man, it's good to see you two—it's been what, three years?"

"Almost four," Jesse offered, "Since we led that group of buffalo hunters out."

James nodded, "I'm glad you made it. By the way," He turned, and gestured to Lucas, who was standing next to a very dissatisfied looking Alfred. "This is

Marshal Lucas Sterling. He's here to haul this... person... back east for trial. Marshal, this is one of my best friends, Sheriff Jesse Molvin, and his wife, Madge."

"Sheriff..." Lucas stepped forward and shook Jesse's hand, "and Ma'am. Nice to meet you both." He gestured to the stage, "I'll go ahead and get this galoot loaded up."

"Travel safe" James offered, and turned back to Jesse. "Now, Jesse, before I put you over in the hotel, there's something I want to ask you about."

***** ******

"Mary?"

At Nate's voice, she looked up from her book. Doc Maggie had left a poetry collection by John Keats, and she'd been reading it, engrossed in a poem about a woman whose older brothers had killed her lover. "Yes?"

"Mary, we need to talk." His voice was low and serious, which set her on edge.

She put the book down, "What's wrong, Nate?"

He leaned forward in his chair, "I can't... well, I've been thinking... I can't do this to you. I want to go to the judge and have him officially annul our marriage."

She came out of her chair like a shot, "What?" She demanded, moving toward him, "What do you mean, you can't 'do this' to me? You mean abandoning us is a

241

better and more noble option?" She poked his chest with her finger. "Why now?"

Nate met her eyes, and she could see the pain there. "Mary, you aren't a criminal, you have a life back in Pennsylvania, a home, friends... and no warrant for your arrest." He shook his head, "And the only thing I have to offer is a life on the run from a noose."

"That's not true!" Mary wanted to scream. She couldn't believe he was doing this now, when everything seemed like it was suddenly going to be alright. "I don't care about those people. We had a plan. We were going west, to California. You won't be found there."

Nate looked at the floor, "When that's the only hope you have, that's an easy hope to hold on to." He shook his head again, "Look, you don't need me. You only married me 'cause it was the best way to hide. You don't need that, and you don't need a husband like me."

She recoiled in anger, "Who are you to tell me what I want or need." She could feel the heat in her face, and knew she should talk quieter, but she needed him to listen. "I chose to marry you, and I choose to stay married to you."

Nate shook his head stubbornly, "I'm not going to do that to you and Clara... Sarah..." He waved with a loud grunt, "See, I never even knew her by her real name. If we get caught together, they might hang you, and take her to some orphanage. That's not fair to either of you." He shook his head again. "I already talked to the Sheriff about the bank. He was going to make inquiries..."

"You told him what you did?" Mary stepped back; her eyes wide with fear. "Why in the world would you do that?"

"Because I did it. It was wrong, and I need to take responsibility for the things I've done wrong." He stood suddenly, his jaw set.

"What about all the good you've done since?" Mary sat on the bed completely aghast, "You saved us, you've..."

"Ran from the law because of what I've done." Nate sighed, "And put you in danger of being an accomplice ever since."

"That's not true..."

"Yes, it is... and that's why I need to go." He turned for the door, but his momentum was suddenly checked at a sudden cry.

"Nate, don't go!" The small voice shocked both of them to silence. Nate turned slowly; his face tight with emotion. Clara was standing on the bed, tears running down both cheeks as she reached out for him. "Don't leave us, Nate."

Mary's chest felt tight as she stared at her sister. It had been so long since she had heard her sister speak that she never really thought of her as listening, but it was obvious that she not only had been listening—but had also understood everything they were saying.

And right then Clara understood that Nate was about to walk out of their lives and didn't like it.

"It's alright Clara. It's ok..." Mary grabbed her sister and pulled her close as she looked over at Nate. He had visibly deflated, and was leaning against the wall by the door, tears running down his own cheeks as he watched Clara. Mary had known for a while that she cared for Nate—how could she not after all they had been through, especially with all that he had done for them—but it was then that she knew she really loved him and didn't want to be without him.

And that she was going to fight for him.

"I have money." She offered as she pulled Clara into a tight embrace.

He stared at her blankly for several seconds, so she added, "I have the house back east, my dad had holdings... a business. Horace didn't drink it all up. We'll hire an attorney... we will fight it."

He shook his head slowly, "I couldn't ask you to do that for me."

"You don't have to..." She was interrupted by an insistent pounding at the door that made her jump.

Nate hurriedly wiped his face and opened the door. The Sheriff standing in the hallway with a crooked smile on his face. "Nate... you sound busy and all, but do you have a moment to talk?"

Nate nodded curtly, "Yes, Sir. Give me a moment." He turned to face Mary and Clara, "I'll be right back, and we'll talk."

Mary tightened her jaw and gave a slight nod. "Alright." And as Nate stepped out, and for the first time in a long time she began praying.

***** ******

SEVENTEEN

Wolcott, WY

Tom Milburne looked up as a boy ran through the door to the saloon and made a beeline for his table. "Mister, I got that message for you." He was holding out a slip of paper like it was a treasure he'd fought for.

Tom stood and took the note from the boy, handing him a two-bit piece in return. "Good job, boy."

The boy ran off, and Tom motioned to the others before he opened the note, scanning the messy scrawl. "They moved Slade again." He read aloud, "Now he's in the cell on the far right of the jail. Not the corner, but the one next to it."

"Is he still alone?"

"Doesn't say, but probably so." Tom sat back in his chair and waved the note at the group, "He wants out tonight though. We need to make sure everything's ready."

Wilfred spat on the ground, "It's all ready, we just need to get it done. We need to get that safe in Rawlings and get out of the area. I got a bounty on my head around here."

"We all got bounties." Miller huffed out a laugh, "Don't act like you're special. Soon as we get that safe, we're heading for Mexico."

Tom rolled his eyes as they continued bickering. He couldn't wait to get this done either, just to be shut of them. He folded the note and scratched at the table with the edge.

"I don't know why we just can't blow it with dynamite," Wilfred complained bitterly. He'd been on a kick about using dynamite since Slade got arrested in Evanston and hadn't shut up about it. He'd been carrying a few dozen sticks in his saddlebags—Tom had no clue where Wilfred had stolen them from—and when no one would agree to abandon Slade and blow the safe in Rawlings, he'd been trying to convince them to use it for the jailbreak.

Purvis spat on the floor, "Fool, Slade's the best yeggman west of the Mississippi and needs his ears to do it—plus that'd make enough noise to wake everyone in town."

Tom shook his head, "No dynamite, so you may as well drop it, Wilfred. We have the plan already. Hostler is gonna have that team of mules yoked and ready come midnight. We'll yank that back wall open a whole lot quieter that way."

Wilfred stood straighter, his hand hovering near his pistol, "You jest watch how you talk to me, boy. I ain't taking none of your lip."

"I think if I were you, I'd consider sitting down..." Tom spoke low and slow. He wasn't scared of Wilfred; he just didn't want to draw attention to them by killing him a few hours before they broke Slade out.

"I ain't scared of you, boy..." Wilfred insisted impatiently, "So, you best watch yourself."

Tom couldn't tell if the man was stupid, or just trying to save face. He didn't care either way. He shifted his leg slightly to get a better angle at his pistol. He knew that even from this position he could draw faster than Wilfred.

"Don't be a fool, Wilfred... sit down." Jefferies spoke quietly from a table nearby where he was playing cards. "You can hate Tom all you want, but you can't beat him... so stop playing games and sit."

That statement took the wind out of Wilfred and he backed off, muttering to himself. Tom watched him closely for a moment to make sure he was done before looking back down at the note. He couldn't wait to get Slade out. He was tired of dealing with these fools, especially Wilfred. What Miller said about Mexico wasn't a bad idea, but it wasn't his plan. He planned to head back east. There were things he wanted to deal with—things he had let slip by for too long.

He shook off the thought and reached for the lamp. The last thing he needed was a suspicious note lying around. He lifted the globe and touched the paper to the flame—it flared brightly for a second and then slowly burned toward his fingers. He stared at the flame and waited until it consumed the entire note. When it was finished, he stood, dropping the charred remains on the floor. He was going to get some rest because it looked like it was going to be a long night.

***** ******

James was silent as Nate followed him across the street to the jail. He didn't know what the Sheriff wanted—surely, he hadn't heard from the judge already.

Had he?

As he stepped through the door, he noticed a man sitting at the Sheriff's desk. Curious, he closed the door behind him, and took off his hat.

"Nate," James started, "I want you to meet a good friend of mine, Jesse Molvin. He came in for the wedding."

Nate stepped forward to greet the man, but he stopped short as the man's eyes fixed on him. He knew those eyes. The last time he'd seen them, the man had been calmly thumbing shells into a pistol—about thirty seconds after gunning Hank down in the bank. He'd spent a lot of time in prayer since Church Sunday and had gotten to the point where he was ready for whatever God had for him. So, he didn't beg or cry, or even try to run. He had scooted as close to God as he could, and now it was time to let God deal with him. Nate took a deep breath, "Well, that was quick, Sheriff."

James chuckled softly, "Have a seat, Nate."

"You want my pistol?" He didn't want to touch it and get shot for the misunderstanding.

"I've got one. Don't need yours." James gestured to one of the chairs, "Sit."

Nate sat and watched Sheriff Molvin. The man seemed introspective and was waiting... but for what?

"So," James started, "Nate, why don't you tell the good Sheriff here what you told me last night."

Nate lifted an eyebrow, "I think he knows."

"Humor me."

Sheriff Molvin's deep voice made Nate jump, but he nodded and took a deep breath. "Alright... well, I rode out through Wyoming earlier this year, and met with these guys in Washakie..." He went through the entire story. He was careful to take accountability for every one of his decisions—he didn't want to be like Jacob any longer—and ended his story when he reached the wagon train.

Sheriff Molvin watched him closely for a moment, "That's not all."

Nate lifted an eyebrow, "What do you mean?"

"Tell me about the wagon train and what's happened since."

Nate threw a glance over at James, who was acting like he wasn't paying attention as he watched a fly crawl around on the ceiling, and continued his story from the wagon, all the way to Cobbinsville.

As he finished the story, there was quiet for a full minute. Finally, Sheriff Molvin grunted and stood to his feet. "Well, nice story." He stretched and looked over at James, "James. I'm sorry, but the kid who robbed our bank died out on the plains. The men from town found the gold—every single Eagle—and we found that bank robber's body there as well... and buried it." He chuckled, "Marker even says 'bank robber.'" He jerked his thumb at Nate, "There was someone else there. Someone that walked out with a woman and a girl, but he wasn't no bank robber." He gave Nate a measured look, "You take care of your wife and little girl now, young man. They're your prime responsibility."

Nate nodded cautiously, not certain if he really understood what just happened. "Yes, Sir."

Sheriff Molvin scratched his nose and sniffed loudly, "Well, James, I'm going over to the hotel to get my Madge and get some grub. I'll talk at you after a bit." With that statement, he put his hat on his head and left the jail.

The door slammed shut, and Nate sat speechless for several seconds staring at it before trusting himself to look over at James. "What was that?"

James chuckled, "That was Sheriff Jesse Molvin. I've known him for upwards of ten years. We fought in the war together, same outfit—me, him, even the Parson—all of us." He waved a hand, "And he's in town now because I invited him to the wedding as my best man." He chuckled softly, "God has a way of working things out for His glory, so when you told me the bank was in Klein, I just figured that was God working— seeming as Jesse was already on the way. I just had to wait for him to get here, and when he did, I asked him about any recent robberies. Well... you see what happened."

Nate looked back at the recently vacated cell area— a place he had resigned himself to staying not ten minutes beforehand—and shook his head as he tried to process the situation. "So, what does this mean?"

James grinned, "Are you thick?" He hooked a thumb at the door, "He said those townspeople think they buried their bank robber. They put a body in a grave that they think was the kid that robbed the bank."

As James continued, all Nate could think about was the dead man at the wagon train with the red plaid shirt. He had unknowingly consigned that man to burial as a criminal.

"...knew that it wasn't the right man, but since you'd dropped the gold to rescue a woman and child..."

"Wait, whoa..." Nate held up his hand, "How could he know that? Did you tell him?"

"Nah, he tracked you. Best tracker around next to..." He grinned, "Well, I guess he might actually be a tad better than me..." He shook his head and pointed at Nate with a serious look Nate knew couldn't be serious, "But don't you dare go around saying such nonsense."

"I won't." Nate stood slowly; his knees weak. He needed to talk to Mary, but he couldn't really believe... He looked at James once more, "But seriously, no jail?"

"Nope." James tilted his head thoughtfully, "Though, I wouldn't plan on visiting Klein in the near future... 'specially not the bank."

"I won't." He gestured to the door, "I need to go."

"Yeah, go talk to your wife. She'll need to know."

"Alright, see you James." He stepped out of the jail, feeling more free than he had for a long while.

***** ******

Nate walked across the restaurant toward the stairwell, pausing briefly to watch Sheriff Molvin and a loud woman he assumed was "Madge" laughing together at a table across the room. Part of him wanted to stop and talk to the man... to explain to the Sheriff how he might have seen what happened as far as Nate's actions, and explain what had been going on in his heart. He wanted to share what Christ had done and how this was a perfect answer to prayer.

The other part wanted to jump on a horse and light a shuck as fast as he could before the man changed his mind, but he controlled that urge and climbed the stairs quickly.

He couldn't wait to see what Mary thought of it all.

***** ******

Mary heard the tread of footsteps on the stairs and dabbed at her eyes with her handkerchief, wishing she could stop the steady flow of tears. She had put on the bold face while she got Clara to settle down after Nate had left, but now that Clara was finally back asleep, she had been alternating between crying and praying. She was certain she looked a fright.

She just hoped it was Nate that was coming and not someone to tell her Nate wouldn't be coming back, but the door opened, and Nate walked through, his face tight with emotion.

Her mind had already raced through a hundred possibilities that ranged from bad to worse. "What did the Sheriff need?"

"He..." Nate blew out a long breath as he closed the door. "He wanted to introduce me to his best man for the wedding."

She cocked her head to the side, "He did what? Why?" Nate had shared with her how strange Sheriff James could be, but that was kind of... unexpected, even from a strange person.

"His best man just came in on the stage." He jerked a thumb toward the window as he sat heavily in the chair, "The same one Alfred left on." The corner of his mouth twitched, and Mary couldn't tell if he was going to cry or laugh.

"I'm sorry, Nate, but I don't understand..."

"I spent all day yesterday, and all through the night praying— waiting for God to tell me what he wanted from me. I had confessed to God that I was like Jacob... that I was wrong, and I wanted to stop being wrong. I just needed Him to show me what He wanted from me."

She found herself nodding slowly, not certain what that had to do with the Sheriff's best man. "OK..."

"I..." He met her eyes, "Mary, I love you. I want to be with you and take care of you and Clara." He moved closer and took both of her hands, "But I couldn't do that with my past hanging over my head." She blanched at his unintended pun, but he continued speaking, his voice low and earnest as he stared into her eyes. "I asked God to show me what He wants in my life, and He just did."

She swallowed with difficulty; her heart felt like it would burst, and she didn't trust herself to speak. She had no idea what Nate was talking about, and it kind of scared her. Was he going to hang, or not?

Nate closed his eyes for a second, and then spoke excitedly, "Sheriff James' best man was also a Sheriff— from a small town in northwest Colorado. Klein."

Mary immediately recognized the name and inhaled sharply, "You mean...?"

Nate nodded slowly. "Yes, and he knew everything already—most of it before James talked to him—even about you and Clara." He shook his head, "Sheriff Molvin had been tracking me, well, he tracked us and knew..." He trailed off in his excitement, his eyes bright with emotion.

"Knew what?" She couldn't understand where he was going with his story.

"Mary, the men from the town got all the gold back and buried someone they thought was me!" He exclaimed with a grin, "Molvin had no intention of correcting them." He blew out a ragged breath, "Mary, I'm free. God did this, I know He did, and I'm free."

Mary was trying to tie the long jumble of words together. "You're not wanted?"

"No, Sheriff Molvin told me point blank that as far as anyone was concerned, I wasn't the bank robber. They don't want me, and they won't ever be looking for me because they already got the gold and buried the robber." He pulled her close, "Don't you see, Mary? I'm free."

Mary finally stopped fighting the tears and let them flow, but they had turned to tears of joy. She returned Nate's embrace as she finally understood, "No, *we're* free."

***** ******

EIGHTEEN

Wolcott, WY

The moon was dipping down toward the horizon when Tom left the saloon. He moved silently through the shadows toward the jail at the edge of town. With the Sheriff playing the shell game with Slade's cell earlier, they wanted to be certain where he was now. His plan was to get in and get out quickly—playing guessing games with the cell would slow them down.

He huffed out a quiet laugh. As if five men moving through the dark with a team of mules wouldn't look suspicious enough, taking them from window to window to see which one Slade was in would be even worse.

It was only a quarter moon, so there wasn't much light, but it was enough to see where he was going... which meant others could probably see him as well. It wouldn't set for another hour or two, so they would have to wait before they pulled this off.

He paused when he reached the building across from the jail and scanned the surrounding streets for movement. Once certain it was clear, he moved around to the back of the building and jogged out into the shadows; circling around to the back of the jail. He had ridden down past the jail that morning to see if there were any dogs in the area that would give them away. Luckily, there was only one—an arthritic hound sleeping on the porch of a house—but it was on the far side of the jail from where he would be going.

He examined the back wall carefully as he stepped closer. It was stone with heavy bars over the windows that were set at least six feet off the ground. He moved under the second window and leapt up, catching the bars easily and pulling himself up. "Slade?" He whispered, hoping there were no guards nearby.

"About time." Slade's voce dripped with annoyance. "Y'all think this is fun, waiting around to be hung?"

"Quit your bellyaching, Slade. We're getting you tonight." He shifted his grip, "You still alone?"

"No, got a cellmate now... He's a dandy." A soft chuckle from Slade was followed by a nasal, whiny voice.

"Would you stop calling me that?"

"Shut up." Slade's sharp retort silenced the dandy's complaint. "Anyway, he's on his way to his own necktie party, so I figgered we'd find some use for him."

"Whatever." Tom really didn't care—his arms were getting tired though. "Be ready to go when the moon drops." He didn't wait for Slade's answer, but dropped to the ground and moved off quickly into the darkness.

***** ******

Cobbinsville, Wyoming

Nate stood quietly by the window, looking out over the empty street. He was still in a state of disbelief and hadn't fully recovered from his talk with the Sheriff earlier. Part of him didn't want to believe it was real and expected to see a posse ride into town to collect him any minute.

But the question on his mind was what to do now. God had obviously worked this out for his glory—he just hadn't showed him what the next step was.

He shifted position slightly and looked down at his bare feet—he'd been walking around the room with his boots off, and when Mary had noticed the large holes in his socks, she demanded he allow her to fix them. He decided to see what she was thinking. "Mary... I was thinking, there's a lot of pretty land here."

Mary looked up from the sock she was darning. "Yes, there is," She offered hesitantly.

"I was just wondering what you... if you..." He trailed off, not really sure he wanted to say anything.

She had stopped and was watching him with interest, "What Nate?"

He tightened his jaw. "I dunno. I was just thinking, the world is open to us right now. I'm willing..." He turned back to the window, "I'm willing to go anywhere you want—I guess I was just wondering what you wanted."

"Nate." She glanced over at Clara, who had fallen asleep on the bed once again, "I honestly don't know. I mean," She let out a quick breath, "Everything that my parents had is back in Philadelphia—their business, their home, everything." She looked down at her lap, "But they are gone, and the only thing for me there is bad memories."

"Horace?" He asked softly.

She nodded slowly, "Yes, I mean, there's no way I could go back to my parents' home. That place... after that..." Her voice started to catch, and she trailed off.

"I understand."

She shook her head, "But it isn't just me either. It's Clara..." She trailed off, looking back over at her sister and chuckled humorlessly, "I can't even remember to call her Sarah anymore." She bit her lip, "But seriously, Horace beat her there, and then..." She met his eyes, "Well, I can never take her back to that house. It would destroy her."

Nate nodded slowly, "I want what's best for you both, and I don't think returning to Philadelphia is it." He took a deep breath, "We still have choices. We can still head to California, or we could even consider staying in this area."

"Well, I will say this." She looked back down at the sock and continued sewing, "You're not going anywhere until I finish these socks—and no amount of staring out the window is going to change it."

He felt his face heat up and sat on the chair. "It still just seems unreal."

"Well, I can certainly understand that, but I plan to just accept the gift that the good Lord has given and move on with life." She lifted the sock up and bit the thread off. "And if He opens an opportunity to move to this area, then we need to think about that—and if He doesn't—then well, we'll just have to see what doors He does open up."

Nate offered a wide smile, "I think that's why I married you. Because you're so brilliant."

Mary looked up with a smile, "No, that was to escape a noose, but you've wised up since then."

They shared a quiet laugh as she set the socks down on the stand and stood, "That said, I think it's time to get some sleep." She gestured to Clara, "Doc Maggie said she should be well enough to travel by the Thursday stage, so we'll talk about it tomorrow."

"Yes, Ma'am." He stood to his feet—it had been an emotionally exhausting day for them both. "Goodnight, Mary."

She crossed the space between them and kissed him on the cheek. "I love you, Nate. I hope you understand that."

Stunned, he looked down into her eyes. "I love you, Mary."

✶✶✶✶✶ ✶✶✶✶✶✶

Wolcott, WY

Wilfred prodded the body with his toe, "Is he dead?" His voice shook as he whispered. "I thought for sure it was a *haint* coming to get me."

Tom gagged on strong smell of whisky that poured off the body lying on the ground. He held his breath as he leaned down and used the man's shirt to wipe the blood off his blade. "Dead now." He stood and snapped his fingers, "Let's move."

They had run across the drunk as they led the mules in a wide circle around town. The moon had almost set; there was just enough light to see where they were going as they moved silently through the dark. He had done everything he could think of to keep the group quiet, including wrapping the trace chains in cloth to keep them from rattling. They had been moving around the town in a wide circle and had almost reached the jail when Wilfred stepped on the drunk's leg. He assumed the drunk had wandered out into the field sometime in the evening hours and passed out—waking up when Wilfred stepped on him. The man had jumped up, hollering unintelligibly, and Wilfred had been so scared that he fell on his backside.

Tom had stepped up and quickly silenced the man with his knife.

Tom scanned the town for movement or light, but there hadn't been any change. Even the arthritic hound hadn't stirred at the drunk's wailing.

They stopped the mule team a few hundred feet outside of town. "Check the chains," Tom ordered the group, "I'm going to be sure it's clear." He grabbed the thick rope and hoisted it onto his shoulder, then crouched into a low run toward the jail. His plan was simple; he would go in, get the rope through the bars for Slade to tie off, and run the line back to the mule team. If everything worked out, he'd grab his horse and the two spares while Purvis hooked the line to the mule team.

And if the Sheriff had a trap set, he'd escape off into the darkness while the others with the mule team tried to escape—he figured they would make so much noise that the posse would follow them instead of trying to find him.

He reached the back of the building and went straight to Slade's window. Dropping the rope, he leapt up and grabbed the bars. "Slade?"

"Hurry up."

The curt answer gave Tom a smile as he dropped back to the ground. He supposed he'd want to hurry up as well. He grabbed the coil of rope, let out a few feet and tossed it up through the bars. As soon as he felt the tug of them pulling on it, he ran back out into the darkness toward the mule team. "Alright," He handed the rope to Purvis, "I'll tug the rope four times in a row. When I do, you get those mules to yank hard."

"Gotcha." Purvis offered simply.

Tom grabbed the reins of his horse from Wilfred and swung up into the saddle. As soon as he was settled, he reached out, "Give me the others." Once he had the other two sets of reins, he rode quickly down to the jail, up to the window. The rope had been looped around the bars several times. "Is it good?"

"It's tight. Let's go."

Tom grabbed the line and yanked hard four times, then spurred his horse. He pulled up a short distance away, just as Purvis's *"Hiyaaa"* sounded from the darkness. There was a groaning noise, then the sound of rocks shifting followed by a loud crashing noise. His horse shied at the noise, but he yanked the reins and spurred the horse toward the jail. He could hear shouts, followed by the baying of a hound as the arthritic dog finally woke up and began letting the town know he was awake.

Tom rode back in quickly, leading the spare horses close as Slade stepped out over the remains of the wall. He grabbed the two sets of reins from Tom. "Got a gun?"

Tom grinned in the dark and pulled his spare pistol from his waistband. He flipped it across the narrow space and turned his horse, spurring it forward without waiting to see if Slade caught the pistol. "Let's go!"

He rode off into the darkness with plans to catch up with everyone later. He wasn't about to risk his neck any further, especially not to make certain the dandy got on his horse. That was on Slade.

***** ******

NINETEEN

Cobbinsville, Wyoming

"We can't leave tomorrow." Mary announced as she burst into the room.

Nate and Clara looked up from his Bible. He'd been reading it aloud to the little girl, trying to work his way through the story of Joseph, but had been struggling with some of the words. He was starting to wish he had paid a tad more attention in school when they were teaching the readin' part. "Sorry, what?"

"We can't leave." She sat down on the edge of the bed, facing them, and the words flowed from her in a steady stream. "I was just talking with Catherine and Doc Maggie, and the Doc had been talking about how great Clara was doing, and how she was ready to travel, and Catherine started to tear up—said that she had assumed we were staying for the wedding—and she was hurt, and I told her that of course we were staying..." She trailed off, looking at him expectantly. "Was that alright?"

Nate grinned, "Of course that's fine. We weren't certain where we were heading yet anyway." He looked down at Clara, "What about you? You in a hurry to go anywhere?"

Clara hid her face in his shoulder. "Stay." Her tiny voice came out muffled, but understandable.

"See." Nate offered, "Even she wants to stay. I'd say you were fine."

"Oh, thank you." Her shoulders slumped in relief and she looked toward the ceiling. "I was hoping you wouldn't mind." She straightened up with a quick smile, "I offered to help with the decorations and anything else that was needed. Catherine's mother will be here tomorrow, and she'll be trying to get everything done before Saturday, and I..." She reddened as she noticed the Bible in his lap and trailed off, "I'm so sorry, I was interrupting you."

"Nah, you're fine." Nate closed the Bible with a soft thump, "I was just practicing my reading skills on Clara, but I think she's 'bout done."

"Are you sure? I mean..."

"Mary, it's fine." He set the Bible on the stand, "And to be honest, James was kind of hinting about us being here for the wedding, so I'm glad something was said." He scratched under his eye with the back of his thumb, "It might hurt his feelings if we don't show."

"Well, we can probably use a man to help with some of the decorations. I don't know what they have planned, but I know Victoria Woodfield, and anything she does will not be simple."

"Alright," He nodded down to Clara whose face was still buried in his shoulder, "But what about her? Is she going to be alright?"

"Doc Maggie said she is fine to be out now." Her mouth curved into a smile, "Matter of fact, I was hoping we could all eat together tonight down at Maude's. As a family."

"That would be nice." His mouth twitched into a teasing smile, "I don't think we've eaten as a family since our wedding night."

"Oh, stop!" She rolled her eyes, "It wasn't like we'd planned it that way."

"I was just funnin' with you." Nate tilted his head, "You think I should check with James, see if he needs anything?" He gave a lopsided grin, "Scattered as he is at times, I don't know if Miss Catherine has him doing anything..."

"Probably not." She leaned forward and whispered conspiratorially, "He's supposed to have picked out a poem to read to her in their vows."

"What's wrong with that?"

She stared at him for several moments before shaking her head. "Never mind. You wouldn't understand." She stood suddenly, "Well, if you want to check with him, that would be fine." She thought for a moment. "And since we're on the topic of staying, we'll need to make arrangements with Miss Maude for the room, at least through Monday."

Nate stood, "I can do that. I wanted to pay her for the last few days anyway. Town shouldn't have to pay for our room since the Marshal finished the investigation."

"Nate!" Clara's tiny voice, sounding affronted, came from the chair they had shared. She was holding her arms out for him to pick her up.

"Well," Nate chuckled as he leaned down and grabbed her, "I s'pose Clara is wanting to go downstairs with me to make those arrangements." His eyes flickered to Mary, "Do you mind?"

"Absolutely not. She'll probably like the fresh air." She looked around the small room, "Well, if you're going to take her, I'll take a few moments to freshen up and change."

"No problem." Nate shifted Clara on his hip, "I may stop by the store while we're down there. I think someone might like some c-a-n-d-y."

Despite his phonetical spelling, Clara gigged loudly and clapped her hands. "Candy!" She exclaimed loudly.

Trying—and failing—to keep a straight face, Mary offered an apologetic smile. "Yeah, Nate... she knows how to spell—and candy is her favorite word."

"That's fine, it looks like we will definitely be stopping now. Take your time." With a quick smile, he and Clara stepped out of the room.

***** ******

TWENTY

Victoria Woodfield took her husbands offered hand and stepped from the stage, looking around distastefully at the small, dusty town. She'd been holding the urge to sneeze since they left the railroad. She couldn't understand why her daughters—both of them now—had chosen to live out here.

"Isn't it wonderful out here, Victoria?"

"Of course, darling." She answered sweetly. Edward was always so adventurous; he had spent the entire trip gushing about how wonderful everything was. She, on the other hand, was holding some stiff reservations. Everything and everyone she met had a distinctly unpleasant odor. She shook off the thought and continued her observation. There were a few buildings on one side of the street, and a decidedly ugly one with a sign that read 'Jail' across from them. Further down she could see a larger whitewashed building that looked like a small Church.

Edward motioned to the store. "At least Theodore's store is easy to find."

"Yes, darling. It is." Of course, with the size of the town, the only difficult thing to find would be a clean place to sit. "Do you think Catherine is there?"

Edward chuckled, "Well, Dearest, I'm not certain; but since we have no idea where to find Theodore and Elizabeth's house, that seems the best place to start." He had just turned to say something to the teamster when a loud voice sounded from behind them.

"Hello there! I'm gonna bet that you're Catherine's parents."

Victoria jumped at the sudden voice and turned to face a tall man that had evidently come out from behind the stage. Her eyes were drawn to the badge on the front of his shirt and she smiled warmly, "And if I were to guess, I would say you are our Catherine's James." She looked him over carefully. He seemed friendly, with a wide grin that was likely infectious to those that knew him. More than that, he looked like someone who could take care of himself—which meant he could take care of Catherine.

She immediately decided that she would like him.

James grin widened, "Yes, Ma'am, I sure am. Did you all have a nice trip?"

Edward stepped past her and offered his hand, "Yes, we did. There's some beautiful country out this way." They shook briefly, and Edward added, "We've been looking forward to meeting you."

James gestured to the store, "Well, Catherine's not at the store—she's down at Ted's house with Elizabeth." He reached for their bags, "Let me get you two settled in the hotel—not that it's a real hotel; Maude lets out a few rooms above the restaurant—but, its real comfortable and it always smells nice. Then I can walk you down to Ted's house... that is, unless you'd rather go to the store and see Ted first."

Victoria nudged her husband's ribs, "No sense in stopping in the store just to see Theodore. Let's drop off our bags at the room and go see our daughters."

Edward grinned, his eyes dancing with amusement—he obviously remembered that she still didn't want to forgive Ted for bringing Elizabeth all the way out here to live. "Yes, Dearest, that sounds wonderful."

James shouldered their large trunk and grabbed a second bag before Edward had a chance to and started towards the restaurant. There was a large sign on the outside welcoming them to 'Maude's'. They hadn't quite made it to the door when Catherine ran up the boardwalk, breathless. "Mother! Father! I am so sorry, I meant to make it here to meet the stage." She grabbed her father in a tight hug before quickly moving to her mother.

"Oh, that's fine, dear." Edward stepped to the side to allow Catherine past him, "We were just getting our luggage to our room."

She embraced her mother tightly, "I'm so glad you made it." She offered brightly as she stepped back. "Maude has your room prepared already." Catherine nodded to James and he moved around the group toward the door. "James will take your bags up, and we can head straight over to Elizabeth and Teddy's."

"I'll be right back," James offered, and disappeared through the door with a quick grin.

Victoria stood quietly as they waited for James. Edward and Catherine kept a steady stream of conversation as Catherine pointed out some of the interesting points of the town: the new Church building down at the end of the street, and the Blacksmith shop that had just put on a new roof—things of small-town interest that she tuned out as she simply scanned the town. There were very few people, and she wondered how Theodore and Elizabeth could possibly make a living here.

The door opened and James stepped out, still wearing a wide grin, "Alright, you're at the top of the stairs, third door down on the right—just past Doc Maggie's room." He offered his arm to her, "Mrs. Woodfield, may I escort you down to Teddy's house?"

She grinned, "Of course," and took his arm. They fell into step behind Edward and Catherine who had continued their stream of conversation as they walked toward Theodore's house. She decided that now would be an opportune time to get some of the answers that Catherine was so willing to avoid answering in her letters. "So, young man. You are the Sheriff of this...

town?" She hated to call it a town—she wasn't certain it even warranted the level of village—but was trying to be positive. "Will that be sufficient to support my daughter?"

Still grinning, James gave her a thoughtful look, "Well, Ma'am, I certainly hope so. I'm not going to lie to you, I am not rich. I have partial interest in a ranch west of here, as well as my income as Sheriff. I wish I could provide her with more—she deserves everything—but we will start simple."

She liked his blunt honesty and nodded in approval. "She's working at Theodore's store, correct? How long is that going to continue?" While helping Theodore out was one thing while she stayed with them, she really didn't want her daughter to be forced into a life of servitude.

James nodded, "She has been, but that will stop after the wedding. I haven't really liked Catherine working at the store, well not since the robbery anyway, and look forward to her just taking care..." James trailed off as she jerked away to face him.

"What do you mean?" Victoria demanded, turning to see his face. She was trying to remain calm, but could hear her voice starting to go shrill, "Robbery? When was this?"

Edward and Catherine had stopped suddenly, and Edward leaned over and patted her arm in a comforting manner, "Oh, I'm sorry love, I didn't tell you. There was a small kerfuffle a few weeks ago... Catherine wrote, but I didn't want to worry you."

Victoria turned and looked at him incredulously, "Kerfuffle?" She shook her head, "You call someone robbing the store our *daughter* was in a kerfuffle?"

James stepped forward, "Well, Ma'am, they didn't actually get far... we stopped them before they took her."

"Took who? Catherine?" Victoria started fanning herself. She suddenly felt feverish and dizzy. "They were trying to kidnap her?"

"Well, yes Ma'am..." James held out his hand in a conciliatory gesture, "But the Parson was right up behind them, and he shot the one..."

"SHOT!" Victoria heard her own voice hit a note it hadn't reached since she was a young girl in her Church choir, "The Parson *shot* someone? Near my daughter?" She looked back and forth between the group. James had stopped talking and was watching her, wide eyed, as if he finally realized he'd said too much.

"Mother, it's alright." Catherine had put a hand on James' arm. "Everything turned out fine."

"Fine? A man was shot near you by a...a..." She sputtered, but couldn't get the word out, "...a Preacher! And you expect me to think everything was fine." She turned on her husband, who was trying to look anywhere else but at her, "Edward. How dare you keep this from me!" She began to fan herself faster. The idea of all of this going on... and she hadn't known. She turned back to face James and opened her mouth to say something; but all that came out was "Oh my!" And everything went dark.

***** ******

"... still shouldn't have mentioned it like that."

"No, James, it wasn't your fault. I should have told her when I heard from Catherine."

At the sound of the voices, Victoria blinked herself slowly awake and found herself staring at a whitewashed ceiling.

"Mother? Are you ok?"

Victoria tilted her head to the side. Catherine was sitting on the edge of a chair next to her bed. She smiled at Catherine's question as she struggled to sit up. "Of course, I am dear. Just a tad... overwhelmed."

Catherine stood quickly and leaned in to help, but her mother waved her off, "I am quite capable of getting myself up." She made it to a sitting position, "I am not feeble, just tired from the journey."

"Yes, mother." Catherine sat back on the edge of the chair, "I'm sorry."

"Oh, it's fine." She waved a hand dismissively, "So, tell me about James. Why him?"

Victoria smiled as Catherine's jaw tightened up—a clear sign she was about to argue—but she held up a finger. "Now, don't get all defensive, I'm just concerned for your safety. I like him much more than that pansy you were seeing before."

Catherine blanched slightly, and Victoria knew it was more than the comparison. "Alfred came here?"

Catherine's head tilted to the side, "You knew he broke out of jail?"

"Yes, but it was just a few weeks ago. We assumed he was just trying to escape and get away." Victoria pursed her lips, "We didn't think he was foolish enough to come after you, especially now that he is wanted for murder as well."

"A little warning would have been nice," Catherine sighed, resting back in her chair.

Victoria watched her daughter closely. She could see something new in her daughter—something Catherine hadn't had before. A resilience, maybe? "Well, I'm sorry... but I see you weren't swayed by his wooing this time."

"Bah!" Catherine's face was a mask of derision. "He grabbed me and shook me like..." She trailed off with a grimace. "I just wish I would have listened to you and father a long time ago."

Victoria struggled to keep the smile from her lips— one of the most thrilling things for a parent to hear was when your children would finally admit you were right. She chose to change the subject, "Is Alfred dead then?"

"Dead?" Catherine lifted an eyebrow, "Not yet—but I daresay that a noose is waiting for him." She shook her head slowly, "No, and I think it took all of James' patience to not hang him here... but he was already in jail when James came back, and the Parson was here..."

"The same Parson that shot someone?" Victoria snorted, "I don't know about this place..."

"Oh mother!" Catherine huffed sharply as she sat back in her chair, "It's not that much different that Philadelphia... better in some ways, since it has given me a more realistic perspective."

"Well, I daresay it's about time for that."

"I'm sorry, mother." Catherine looked down at her lap, "Looking back, I can see my own ignorance and immaturity—I wish I would have seen it sooner—but then again, Parson William says that hindsight is always clearer."

Victoria scoffed, "Well, at least he has some sense to go with the gun he carries. That gives me hope." She stood slowly, waving off Catherine's attempt to assist. "Young lady, I am not an invalid. I just had a scare— thanks to you I might add—but I'm over it now. I'm ready to join the others."

"Are you certain, mother?"

"Yes—I don't suppose that Parson of yours is around though? I should like to meet him as well."

"I'm sorry, mother, but I'm afraid that he doesn't live in town. His ranch is several miles outside of town." She gave a bright smile, "But he should be in tomorrow, and you can meet him then."

"That will be fine." She gestured toward the door, "I suppose we should go out and see the others, that way they can stop whispering and fussing. I need to see my other daughter, and then..." She feigned a chill, her mouth crinkling as she held back a smile, "I want to look at these wedding plans. Heavens knows what horrific things you all have come up with."

"Oh, mother! Stop." Catherine grabbed her mother in a tight hug, "I'm so glad you're here."

"So am I, sweetheart." Victoria patted her daughter's back. "So am I."

***** ******

"Well, James," Nate mused as he peeled a short piece from his chunk of wood, "You don't seem to be nervous. I'd have thought with the wedding tomorrow, you'd be a little worried."

James shrugged absently as he peeled another layer of thin wood from his stick. He was trying to show Nate how to properly whittle, but he hadn't been able to make much more than toothpicks. "Nah, not so much." He looked up at Nate, "Were you nervous when you got hitched?"

Nate tilted his head thoughtfully, "No, sir. I guess it was a bit too fast—and it wasn't like a real wedding then, you know, so I s'pose that was different." He turned red and looked back down at the piece of wood he was whittling. "I mean, I liked her, and I was making a commitment, but I didn't have a bunch of time to overthink it and get nervous."

James nodded, "Kinda like the difference between marching into a battle and someone pulling a gun on you in the street."

"Yes, sir. That's probably it." Nate looked back up, "Have you made plans for after the wedding?"

"Well," James shrugged, "I wanted to travel a bit. I know it's nothing compared to Philadelphia, but I wanted to take her to Cheyenne, and maybe even Denver—see some of the things she missed coming straight to Cobbinsville like she did."

Nate grunted, "Sounds like a fun trip. Gonna be gone long?"

"Nah." He shaved off another layer, "Little over a week. Ted and Earl are gonna help keep an eye on the town." He chuckled for a moment, "Not that Earl needs an excuse to be in town much."

They shared a quiet laugh and continued whittling. James pulled his stick up to eye level and looked at it skeptically, "How about you? Have you decided when you was leaving?"

"Well..." Nate offered hesitantly, "We've been talking. Clara is past the bad spell. We had originally talked about leaving yesterday, but then your fiancé went and roped Mary into staying for the wedding." He clucked his tongue, "But we really weren't certain anyway. Right now, I suppose we're just waiting on the Lord to give some direction."

James worked to keep a smile from his face, "How does the missus feel about going back?"

"Well, to be honest, Mary doesn't really want to go back to Philadelphia. Nothing but bad memories there, really." Nate eyed his piece of wood for a second, then held it out for James to inspect, "Like that?"

James frowned at the small dog the kid had whittled. It looked good, but he wasn't about to tell him that. "Head's a little misshapen."

"Oh." Nate nodded and started working on the dog's head again. "Well, we talked about going on to California like we originally planned, but I dunno." He leaned forward a bit, looking up the trail. "Rider coming into town."

James tilted his head, "Yup, looks like the good Marshal is back for the wedding. Doc'll be pleased."

They shared a laugh and continued whittling as the Marshal rode up to the jail and stopped at the hitching post. "James, Nate."

James looked up with a wide grin, "Marshal Sterling! I expected you on the stage yesterday. I was beginning to think you weren't coming back."

Lucas shook his head gravely as he stepped down from his horse. "I didn't think I was going to make it back at all, James." He tied the reins to the post and turned to face them. "Had a jail break up in Wolcott. Leader of a small gang was on his way east for trial— murder. Rest of his gang came and broke him out. They killed someone in the process."

James stood, dusting the wood shavings from his lap. "Did you catch them?"

"No," Lucas grabbed his saddlebags and mounted the steps, "They're still on the loose. But, there's a snag—they took Alfred with them."

Frowning, James folded his knife and stuck it in his pocket. "Alfred? Why would they take him?" He looked up the street, as if he expected Alfred to be riding in behind the Marshal. "Do you think they are coming here?"

"I can't imagine why. Alfred was a two-bit crook with no talents this gang could use. They probably took him out of pity since he was going east to hang." Lucas shook his head, "However, just in case Alfred breaks off from the rest and tries to come back to town..." He offered a weak grin, "I wanted to be here for the wedding."

James chuckled humorlessly. He was glad to see the Marshal but wasn't thrilled about Alfred being free. He knew he should have just hung Alfred himself and been done with it. "Well, Marshal, you may as well go ahead and bunk here at the jail with me. Maude's will be full up between Catherine's family and the Parson." He glanced over at Nate, "Well, and the Taylor's as well, I suppose."

"Thought you forgot about me, James." Nate offered a grin and turned to the Marshal. "Despite the circumstances, its good to see you, Marshal."

"You as well, Nate." Lucas moved past them to the door, his face turning a light shade of pink, "Well, gentlemen, I'm going to drop my gear off and step across the street to see... someone."

James looked over at Nate as Lucas disappeared into the jail. "I do believe that young man is heading to see our doctor."

"And he's not even sick." Nate shook his head, "You worried about Alfred?" He asked quietly.

"Nah." James pulled his knife back out of his pocket and sat, "I'll just get to shoot him this time." He picked up a chunk of wood, "Now, where were we?"

***** ******

TWENTY-ONE

By Saturday afternoon it looked like every person that lived within a hundred miles had arrived in Cobbinsville. James peered at the busy street through the small window of the Parson's office—he was waiting there for the wedding to start—and it seemed like everyone he'd ever met decided to come see him get hitched.

"Lot of people in town today, isn't there?" James frowned as he spoke. He hated how he could hear the shakiness in his own voice. He turned from the window and pulled at his collar.

Earl chuckled softly, "You know why, don't yeh? It's 'cause Catherine done shot you once already." At James' horrified look, he added, "They're here to see if'n she was going to do it again."

"They are not!" James grabbed his hat—the first thing he could get ahold of—and chucked it across the room at Earl. "You just get out of here if yer going to start trouble."

Earl looked over at Thomas, who was sitting quietly by the wall watching them both. "He just doesn't like to hear truth, does he, Thomas?"

Thomas looked thoughtful, "I dunno, Mr. Earl. I don't reckon anyone expects Miss Catherine to shoot Mr. James again."

"See, you old scallywag," James offered triumphantly, "Told you."

Chuckling, Earl walked to the door, "Alright, but you just watch yourself when you're up there. If you hear a shot..." He trailed off dramatically and left the room.

James frowned at the door, "She's not going to shoot me." He spoke quietly, more to reassure himself. He was pretty sure she didn't even have a gun on her.

Of course, with Alfred on the loose again...

He shook off the thought and pulled nervously at the collar of his suit again. He hated wearing his suit. It was hot and itchy; even his Sunday go-to-meetin' clothes weren't this uncomfortable. Matter of fact, he could count on one hand the number of times he'd worn a suit and hadn't been planning to add to that number.

Part of him wondered if he would have still asked Catherine to marry him if he'd have remembered he had to wear a suit. His brow furrowed in consternation; he hadn't worn the blessed thing since he'd packed it away after his Ma's funeral—and hadn't planned on wearing it again until his own.

He stopped at that thought and turned to Thomas, "Hey, Thomas... you want to do me a quick favor?" He whispered some quick instructions to the young boy.

Thomas lifted an eyebrow, "Are you sure, Mr. James?"

"Yes, please. And hurry. We ain't got a lot of time before this thing starts."

He watched Thomas run from the room, hoping the boy would be discrete. "I'll show him." He muttered as he turned back to the window. Another cart was rolling into town. Great.

"Are you alright, James?"

James turned in surprise at the voice. The Parson had stepped into the room, and was standing a few feet away, grinning as he looked him up and down. "You look pretty nervous there."

James reddened slightly, but rolled his eyes, "Nah, I'm not nervous. I just can't wait to get out of this blasted suit."

"Well," Parson William raised an eyebrow, "You may want to at least wait until after the ceremony is over for that, else people might talk."

James glared at him, "Well, of course. I just want to hurry up. How much longer are the womenfolk gonna take?"

"Let's see," Parson William pulled his watch from his pocket, "The ceremony begins at two-o'clock. It's one forty-three right now." He looked up, "I'd say, probably six hours before the women are ready."

"Six hours?" James stared wide eyed for several seconds before he realized Parson William was joking. "Don't do that to me, Parson. You know I can't take this much longer."

Parson William grinned, "You'll be fine, James. Is there anything else you need?"

James looked around the room, "No, not really. Everything else has been done by the womenfolk." He focused back on Parson William, "No sign of Alfred, right?"

"Neither hide nor hair. I think he's too smart to come back here, given his previous experiences in town." Parson William grinned as he gestured to the door. "There's not a soul out there that wouldn't..." He trailed off with a shake of his head, "Well, let's just say that if he shows up, his reception will be harsh."

"Fair enough, Parson. Catherine's not concerned either, so I s'pose we're all good." He cocked his head to the side, "Do you s'pose there's still plenty of food? I was worried after seeing all these visitors ride in, unexpected like." He shuddered, glad that Ted had offered to pick up the tab for the food. With all the unexpected guests that showed up, he'd been worried that they were going to run out of food—especially since old Isaiah Henry and his wife Millicent had ridden in.

"I'm sure there's enough." Parson William offered a comforting smile. "You good then?"

"Well, Parson—I s'pose I have everything I need." He patted his pockets, "Wait, what did I do with that ring?" He had ordered a really fancy ring from the store—paid a whole two month's salary for it. Of course, he had no idea what a woman would think was fancy, so he'd had Elizabeth and Anna help pick it out from the catalog—he figured that since they seemed to think it was nice Catherine would as well.

Now where did he...

Parson William sighed, "Thomas has the ring, he's the ring-bearer...remember?" He gave James a close look, "You sure you aren't nervous?"

James shook his head, "No, I'm not nervous. I just forgot." He frowned and gestured around the room, "I had too much stuff to take care of, so I forgot."

Parson William's eyes danced in amusement, "You had to get dressed, James. That was pretty much all of it." He shook his head, "But, ok. Long as you don't forget your lines."

James patted his pocket, "I've got that written down here. I was going to read her a poem, like you suggested." At the Parson's sharp look, he added, "No, not Keats. I picked something better."

When Catherine had suggested him reciting a poem during his vows, he had thought about doing something by Keats since all the womenfolk had seemed to be enamored with his poetry here of late. But when he had mentioned it to the Parson, the Parson about had a fit.

Parson William checked his watch one last time, "Ok..." He tilted his head to the side, as if about to ask a question, but shook his head. "Well let's get ready to go then." He looked around, "Where did you send Thomas off to?"

James felt himself go a deep shade of red, "He just had to go pass a message, that's all. He'll be back any..." He trailed off as Thomas reappeared at the door with Jesse Molvin.

Jesse coughed, "It's one fifty-five, Parson. Womenfolk want you in position."

Parson William clapped James on the shoulder, "Alright James, see you inside." The Parson left the room, and James immediately turned to Thomas. "Did you...?"

Thomas gave a salute, "I asked, sir. She told me that she left it at the store."

At Jesse's confused look, James nodded slowly as a wide grin crossed his face. "Now I'm ready."

***** ******

Nate gripped Mary's hand tighter as he shifted uncomfortably in the pew, once again resisting the urge to look behind him at the growing crowd. James had asked them to sit up at the front with the close friends and family, but he hated sitting up front, especially with everyone filing in behind him. He suspected James just did it to see him squirm at the front of a Church again.

He took a deep breath and focused on the soft strains of music—the Parson's wife was playing a slow tune on the cello as people entered, and the gentle music was somewhat calming. He glanced down at Clara, who was sound asleep with her head resting on his leg. He huffed out a quiet laugh; the music had already lulled the little girl to sleep.

Biting his lip, he looked around the sanctuary. The decorations were beautiful. He had read to Clara while Mary had helped Doc Maggie, Elizabeth, and the Parson's wife, Anna, with the lavish decorations. They had done a beautiful job in the short amount of time that they'd had. He squeezed Mary's hand, and leaned closer. "I wish our wedding could have been this nice," He offered quietly.

He jumped at a sharp pain in his shoulder, Mary had punched him and was staring at him with a mischievous grin on her face.

"What?" He asked, rubbing his shoulder in mock pain.

Mary leaned closer and whispered, "Our wedding was wonderful. Decorations are nice, but they aren't everything." She kissed him on the cheek and sat back.

He grinned back, "Well, yes Ma'am..."

She suddenly gripped his hand tighter, "There's James and Sheriff Molvin. It must be about to start!"

Suddenly, the music changed to a strident march. Nate turned slightly and looked to the back of the Church. The Parson's son, Thomas, was slowly escorting a little girl up the aisle. She was dropping flower petals on the floor as they moved up the aisle toward the front. He could see Catherine in the vestibule, ready to come in.

Mary's fingers clenched his even tighter, "There she is."

As Catherine and her father started down the aisle, the audience stood in respect as they passed. Nate shifted Clara from his lap and stood as the bride passed them. He looked down at Mary, who had tears streaming from her eyes as she watched Catherine pass.

Nate felt his chest tighten, but he knew that the emotion he felt had nothing to do with Catherine and James, but because of his own bride. He couldn't believe how lucky he was to have her. He leaned close and whispered, "Mary, I love you."

***** ******

James has been standing facing the Parson with his eyes closed while waiting for Catherine's entrance. Her mother had warned him that if he turned around, or even opened his eyes, before the march began, she would skin him alive in front of everyone.

And he had believed her, which is why his eyes were still closed.

"James, get ready to turn." Jesse whispered hoarsely.

James opened his eyes, just as Parson William nodded for him to turn. He took a deep breath and turned—and almost passed out. It was like he was in a tunnel—the music and everything that was going on were suddenly muted in the background—and all he could see was Catherine walking slowly down the aisle, clutching her father's arm. She was beautiful—more beautiful than he'd ever seen her, which was saying something.

He couldn't move, couldn't even breathe as he watched her getting closer, finally stopping a few feet away. Her smile was radiant. What seemed like a hundred miles away, Parson William asked, "Who gives this woman away today?"

"Her mother and I," was the response someone nearby gave. Suddenly, Catherine moved forward a step and put out her arm for him to take.

He grabbed her arm and started heading for the door, but Jesse clapped a hand on his shoulder, and whispered, "You've got to wait for the ceremony."

James shook himself, and everything suddenly snapped into focus—he could hear someone giggling in the audience and realized that he had messed up. "Yeah, sorry." He grinned apologetically at Catherine and stepped closer to the Parson.

Parson William's mouth twitched in a half smile, and he looked past them to the audience. "We are gathered here together in the sight of Almighty God to witness this union between James and Catherine..." The Parson's voice slowly faded into the background as James stared into Catherine's face. He could not believe that God had blessed him with someone so beautiful, both in spirit and in her looks. She could have had anyone in the universe, but she had chosen him. She actually chose him. Sure, she shot him, and hit him with a few dozen things, but that wasn't bad, was it. It wasn't like she was going to do it again. He glanced down at her dress—he didn't think she could even hide a pistol in that dress, plus Thomas had asked, and she said she didn't have it on her. Besides, there was no...

His thoughts were interrupted as Catherine jerked his hand and motioned to the Parson with her head. He looked over at the Parson, who was watching him expectantly.

Parson William smiled, "James Abraham Matthews, do you take this woman, Catherine Bertha Woodfield, to be your lawfully wedded wife...?"

"Yes." James blurted loudly. There were some titters of laughter behind him, but he stayed focused on the Parson's face. He couldn't look at Catherine, because he was afraid that he'd just messed something up.

Parson William cleared his throat and continued, "...To love, honor and cherish; forsaking all others; to have and to hold in sickness and in health, as long as you both shall live?"

There was a long pause. James continued to study Parson William, who in turn was watching him expectantly. Parson William finally quirked an eyebrow. "Well, James, do you?"

James was confused, "Do I what?"

Parson William took a deep breath and closed his eyes, "Take Catherine..."

James frowned, "Didn't I just say..." He trailed off at the sharp look from the Parson. "Yes, yes I do." He tried to remember—he was pretty sure this was where he was supposed to read his poem. He coughed, as he pulled the paper from his pocket. He had spent a lot of time carefully copying it from the book and hoped she liked it.

He looked at Catherine, and then read slowly;

"Yes, Love indeed is light from heaven;

A spark of that immortal fire

With angels shared, by Alia given,

To lift from earth our low desire.

Devotion wafts the mind above,

But Heaven itself descends in Love..."

He trailed off and looked back up at Catherine. Tears were running from her eyes, but she was smiling. "That was beautiful, James." She mouthed quietly.

He smiled and folded the paper back into his pocket. He was just glad she liked it—Earl had acted like he couldn't pick out a poem to save his life. He grinned and faced Parson William who nodded to James' right. James looked down; Thomas had stepped between him and Jesse and was holding out the ring. He took it and turned to Catherine.

The Parson asked, "James, do you give this ring as a symbol of your constant faithfulness and abiding love to Catherine?"

"I do." He put the ring on Catherine's finger, thankful that it slid on easily.

Parson William nodded and turned to Catherine. "Do you, Catherine Bertha Woodfield, take this man, James Abraham Matthews, to be your lawfully wedded husband? To love, honor, and obey; forsaking all others; to have and to hold in sickness and in health, as long as you both shall live?"

Catherine focused her eyes on James, "I do." She smiled, and started to quote from memory;

"A thing of beauty is a joy for ever:

Its loveliness increases; it will never

Pass into nothingness; but still will keep

A bower quiet for us, and a sleep

Full of sweet dreams... and quiet breathing.

An endless fountain of immortal drink,

Pouring unto us from the heaven's brink."

She finished the poem and finally broke eye contact to look back at Parson William.

Parson William asked, "Catherine, do you give this ring as a symbol of your constant faithfulness and abiding love to James?"

"I do." She pulled James' hand up and slid the ring onto his finger.

Parson William nodded once more. "For as much as James and Catherine have consented in holy wedlock, and have thereto confirmed the same by giving and receiving each one a ring; by the authority committed unto me as a minister of Jesus Christ, I now declare you husband and wife, according to the ordinance of God, and the laws of the state of Wyoming; in the name of the Father, and the Son, and the Holy Spirit, Amen." He looked down at James, "James, you may now kiss your bride."

***** ******

TWENTY-TWO

"Come on, Clara, you can take a bite. My momma made it, and it's good." Little Sarah Mae Nunn and the Parson's son, Thomas, were both trying—unsuccessfully so far—to coax Clara into eating a piece of the chicken that Sarah Mae's mother had brought for the wedding supper.

"Do you think they'll get her to eat?" Nate asked casually. He and Mary were sitting at the other end of the table as they watched the trio.

"She'll eat chicken sometimes." Mary chuckled, "But it might be that she just likes the attention."

Nate nodded as he took a small bite from his plate, and gestured with his fork, "You really ought to try Mrs. Barlowe's pie."

"I think I've eaten too much as it is." Mary leaned forward, her nose crinkling in distaste, "Besides, isn't that gooseberry?"

Nate shrugged as he jammed another bite into his mouth, "Not sure, but it's tasty," He answered around the bite.

"Close your mouth," Mary giggled, tossing a napkin at him, "The Parson's coming over to talk."

Nate grinned and took the final bite of his pie as the Parson and James' brother Earl walked up to the table.

The Parson nodded down the table at the three kids, "Looks like them two took on a challenge there."

"She's a picky eater, Parson." Mary offered. "Have a seat. Nate would offer, but his mouth is full."

"Thank you." The Parson grinned as he and Earl sat down. "Children are a blessing; that is certain." He focused on Nate, "So, Nate, I know it's been a stressful week and a half for you two, but I wanted to see if you and your wife have decided what you are going to do now?"

Nate glanced sideways at Mary before answering. That was the one question everyone had been asking—and he had been avoiding—since they still hadn't decided where they were going to go. "We've been talking about it." He hedged.

The Parson nodded, "Well, that's a decision that you both need to be praying carefully about." He gave Earl a sideways glance, "But it might help if you know what options you have."

Nate tilted his head curiously, "Options, Parson?"

The Parson shrugged, "Earl's been talking about moving off his ranch. He doesn't want to admit it, but he's getting old."

"Seasoned, Parson... not old," Earl corrected with a broad grin.

"Sorry, Earl. I meant seasoned." The Parson shook his head, "Point is, James' seems to like you—thinks you have good character..." At Nate's lifted eyebrow the Parson waved a hand dismissively, "I know what you're thinking, but there's more to life than worrying about past mistakes. It just so happens that God is giving you an opportunity to make up for that mistake—which is more than many people get."

Earl broke in, "So, the point is, I'm thinking about selling out, and thought I'd give you first dibs. I'd let you pay it off over time, but I'm done, and James isn't rancher material, so he won't take over. As the Parson said, you earned his respect—we both feel we could trust you." He nodded toward Mary, "Ma'am, I know you have some holdings back east, and if'n your goal is to get back to that, no problem. But, just in case you liked it in these parts, we might work something out."

Nate looked back and forth from the Parson to Earl, then finally back to Mary. "I don't know what to say. I mean..." He shrugged, utterly lost for a response.

"Nothing to say right now. Just think about it." Earl offered, gesturing to Clara, "Doc said the little girl is ready to travel, but that doesn't mean you have to make any decisions yet. You can stick around—give her a bit longer to heal up whilst you think about it. I'm not in a hurry." He gestured to the setting sun, "Ranch is out that way a piece... little over halfway to the Parson's place. You can ride out with me sometime this week if'n you want. See it firsthand."

Nate glanced at Mary, "Well, we will certainly pray about it, Earl, but whatever our decision, we want you to know that the offer is appreciated."

"No problem at all." Earl stood, "Now, I'd love to stay and chat longer, but I see that some of the other guests aren't socializing." He tipped his hat toward Mary, "Ma'am..." and moved off through the crowd.

The Parson smiled broadly, nodding in the direction Earl had taken. "As I said, Earl wants to move to town." He shook his head, "So, while he socializes with miss Maude, I need to speak to a few more people before James and Catherine leave." He stood from his seat, "So, either way, I'll see the three of you in Church tomorrow, right?"

Nate stood up, offering his hand. "You sure will, Parson."

As the Parson walked off, Nate sat back down, his face flushed. "What do you think?"

Mary looked at him, her eyes bright with excitement. "To be honest, I don't know." She shook her head slowly, "I just know that a few weeks ago I had no idea what to do, but I felt lost and alone." She reached out and took his hands, "Now, I still don't know what to do, but I don't feel lost or alone."

Nate leaned forward, pressing his forehead to hers. "That's because you're not alone, Mrs. Taylor."

***** ******

EPILOGUE

Tilman Boster stepped off the train and took a deep breath. He loved how fresh the air was; he had been cooped up in the city for so long that he'd forgotten the clean smell.

He glanced up at the low setting sun. It was probably too late for a stage—the office was probably closed as well, but he could check after he got a room. He spotted a sign announcing a hotel only a block up from the train station. Close enough to walk. He grabbed his bag and marched toward the hotel. He was hoping to get a room, then get some supper and a good night's rest before starting the long trip by stage tomorrow. He was looking forward to seeing his daughter; it had been years, too many long years, and now...

"Hey, Mr. What are you doing? That's mine."

Tilman felt himself shoved from the back suddenly and stumbled forward a few steps, dropping his valise to the ground. He turned, surprised as he was faced by a roughly dressed man. "Excuse me?"

"I said that's mine!" The man yelled; he had his hand poised by his pistol.

Tilman stepped back and lifted his hand, thoroughly confused. He looked to his left and right; everyone was slowly backing away from the scene. Was this a mistake? He focused back on the man, "I'm sorry, sir, I do not understand what you are talking about."

"You're a thief, I say!" The man yelled and drew his gun.

Tilman felt the impact of the slug before he heard the shot. He stumbled back, and then slumped to the ground, clutching his stomach. Rough hands shoved him onto his back and rifled through his coat.

The man stood, holding something aloft, "See, this is mine. He tried..."

The man's voice faded as Tilman stared at the sky. The last thought he had before losing consciousness was of his daughter.

***** ******

Marshal Lucas Sterling stared at the man in the bed, "So, he was unarmed?"

The doctor nodded, "Yep, and robbed from the looks of it." He shook his head, obviously disgusted,

"Fine time for it too. Sheriff was stove up. He done fell off his horse yesterday."

"No deputies?" Lucas asked quietly.

"Nah, they were out of town." He shook his head again, "Yep, the robber just started yelling at this man and said something was his, then he pulled out his gun and shot." He looked over at Lucas, "My wife was there, she said he pulled a wallet from the man's coat and showed everyone in the crowd, told them it was his."

Lucas chewed on his lower lip, "Nobody stopped him?"

The doctor shook his head, "Nah, about that time there were two more in the crowd that started arguing and threatening to shoot each other. By the time they stopped, the man had disappeared."

"Likely working together," Lucas nodded to himself, "I've seen it before." He blew out a short breath in frustration, "So, do we have a name for the shooter, or on the victim?"

"Names..." The doctor tilted his head to the side, "One of the two others called the shooter Ted... several witnesses said that. Plus, my wife mentioned that one of the other two... the one feller—he was a little..." He whistled, "You know. A real dandy. She thought he matched a wanted handbill she read just yesterday. Alfred, I think his name was."

Lucas pulled a handbill from his pocket and opened it up, "This one?"

"Yessir," The doctor nodded vigorously, "That'd be him. Alfred Beachem. Said he's a real dandy." He tilted his head, "She wasn't worried about any reward though. Just seeing justice."

Lucas rubbed his jaw slowly. He hated that Alfred was still on the loose. Part of him felt guilty for going down to Cobbinsville to see James and Catherine's wedding—maybe if he hadn't gone, he would have already caught Alfred, and this wouldn't have happened.

Of course, if he wouldn't have gone to Cobbinsville, Alfred may have showed up there and caused trouble. Six of one half-dozen of the other.

"Come to think of it..." The doctor muttered, "The victim..." He leaned over and grabbed an envelope from the dresser. The bottom corner was stained with blood. "Victim had this in his pocket; I assume it's addressed to him."

Lucas accepted the envelope and scanned the name of the addressee, "Tilman Boster?" He muttered quietly. That name didn't ring a bell. Then he glanced at the addressor and inhaled sharply. "That's not good."

The letter was posted from Parson William Stone.

***** ******

About the Author

STEVE C. ROBERTS lives in Central Missouri with his wife and four children. He is a professional teacher and counselor, and has spent the last twenty years as a Volunteer Chaplain for the Department of Corrections. He also serves in various other capacities in his home Church. His writings include several Non-fictional devotionals as well as several Christian Fiction novels, including the Men of the Heart series.

Made in the USA
Middletown, DE
27 February 2022

61905111R00194